CHOCOLATE
HEARTS
AND MURDER

Book Two: The Fiona
Fleming Cozy Mysteries

PATTI LARSEN

ACKNOWLEDGMENTS

With my deepest thanks to:

Jessica Bufkin
Christina G. Gaudet
Scott Larsen
Kirstin Lund
Lisa Gilson Noe
Caron Prins

From the bottom of my heart, for saying yes.

CHAPTER ONE

WHY WAS IT FANCY Valentine's Day drinks were always tinted red? Reminded me more of gore and mayhem than anything to do with romance. Which said a lot, I suppose, for my state of mind when it came to relationships and dating.

No bitterness in Fiona Fleming toward the opposite sex or anything.

I sipped carefully at the wildly inappropriate mimosa the bartender smilingly handed me and shrugged off the sweetness. It had alcohol in it, so I guess it would do. A few of these and I might even find a way to enjoy myself tonight. Yeah, right.

Don't get me wrong. It was kind of a big deal to be invited, from what I understood, to Mayor Olivia Walker's extra special, don't you dare miss it, White Valley Ski Lodge Resort Extravaganza and fashion show. Snort. I tipped my glass to a pair of young women I didn't know out of the need to at least appear friendly and perused the bar where I hoped to spend the bulk of tonight before returning to my room and hiding out there until I could go home.

My free hand tugged at the short hemline of the dress Daisy picked out for me while I did my damnedest not to show how uncomfortable I was in the shining satin sheath. No one told my best friend that redheads look terrible in crimson. Though, as it turned out, this particular dress's color actually complimented my thick, auburn hair, matched to the deep red lipstick she insisted I wear. The kind of "lasts all night and won't kiss off" stuff she knew was my only hope for keeping color on my lips due to my utter lack of giving a crap about makeup.

Smart girl, that Daisy. Not that I was going to be kissing anyone. But a girl could hope.

Maybe I could carve out a little corner by the bar here, in the dim light of the long, narrow space with the lovely music piping through in tasteful strains of reworked pop songs, (sarcasm, check) while water cascaded in enthusiastic downfall over the glass feature that was the back wall. The slick marble tiles were a bit treacherous underfoot, made worse by the heels Daisy forced on my feet. Come to think of it, I'd been worried they'd be hurting by now, laughed at her when she insisted on taping my toes together, only to discover she knew what she was doing and that my tender, sneaker favoring tootsies actually felt all right.

I spotted Olivia across the room and ducked my head, the updo making it impossible to hide behind my hair like I usually did. Damn Daisy and her deft fingers, though I had to admit the final result— makeup, dress, shoes and hair—left me a little breathless and willing to at least date myself. I turned toward the bar, the mirror behind it reflecting her artwork, and grinned for a second at just how hot I actually looked.

Now, if only I wasn't the only woman here under thirty who was single... not fair. I was sure it only felt that way. And nice to have an excuse to do something on Valentine's Day that had nothing to do with men or pretending they weren't all jerks. Still, I watched Olivia in her pale cream gown making her rounds, all poised politician perfection, and my grin turned to a grimace. I'd let her bully me into this, just like I'd allowed it the last eight months since I took over my Grandmother Iris's B&B, Petunia's. From the moment she intervened with the sheriff over the death of Pete Wilkins and kept my business open, murder or no murder, the woman seemed to think she owned me. And the rest of the town.

Mind you, she was doing a stellar job of putting our sleepy little Reading, Vermont on the map of must visit places in the continental US. Savvy didn't begin to describe her ability to wrangle press and attention and everyone thrived thanks to it. But there were times it rankled.

Like three weeks ago when she showed up in the foyer of Petunia's, patted my pug of the same name on the head (a prerequisite for anyone wishing to spend even five seconds at the B&B) and then informed me in no uncertain terms with the faintest lines of tension and tiredness for her relentless campaigning finally showing around the edges that I was attending tonight's little soiree.

No luck hiding from her either now that I was here, it turned out. With her carefully cultivated welcoming smile plastered on her olive skinned face, makeup professionally applied and hair glossy in the low light, Olivia took time out of her busy schmoozing schedule to swoop across the bar and pounce. That is, spend a moment with me.

"A smile would be lovely," she said through her own beaming expression, tone not matching her lips or joy reaching those dark eyes. The hints of exhaustion hadn't left her. She really needed to take a break from all her hard work at some point. "For the good of Reading." That elegant pause, weighted with guilt, was by now classic Olivia Walker, boss of everyone. "You *do* want our town to continue seeing success, don't you, darling Fiona?"

No use arguing. I did agree with her, just wasn't all that keen on being a show pony in her particular three ring circus. "I'm here, aren't I?" Okay, so not very gracious, but no one ever accused me of being over enthusiastic when I was pinned to the wall.

"Listen," she leaned in with that smile turning to a tight, feral snarl, dark eyes snapping, weariness gone in favor of intensity, "I saved you when Pete Wilkins died and don't you forget it. You owe me, Fiona."

"You kept Petunia's open," I snapped back. "Which, technically is a place, Olivia. I'm a person."

"Not to me." Because, to Olivia Walker I was nothing to her without Petunia's.

While I was aware of that fact, she'd never come out and said it in so many words. At least I knew where I stood. I grit my teeth and bit the bullet. Of course I did. While Olivia strolled off, smiling and nodding like she hadn't just handed me my self-esteem on a platter.

Turning away again seemed the best, if miniscule, revenge. I glanced at the clock behind the bar, hating that I fretted. There was a time I could have cared less about time or anything outside my own little world. But pondering Petunia's made me think about the two elderly ladies who I'd left in charge back in town. While I was only a fifteen minute drive from the B&B, it felt like a million miles. Now, Mary and Betty Jones had taken excellent care of Petunia's when my grandmother had her stroke, worked there for years before that, handled everything with their stolid determination and quiet grumpiness I knew now came from natural stoic natures and not from actual dissatisfaction. Still, it was one of the busiest nights of the year. The news channel's perky weather girl had been warning all day about the possibility of snow tonight, too. Could they deal with snow? Fee, seriously. The pair had spent their entire lives in a mountain town. Snow was nothing to them. But they had been left in charge of dinner and the music and...

I really needed to call them. Check in. Not because I wanted a distraction from standing alone at the bar with a decidedly Valentine's Day drink in my hand, a room in the brand new resort waiting for me upstairs, a free dinner pending and no one to share it with.

Right.

Just when I thought tonight couldn't get any worse, well. It got worse. Right about the same instant Vivian French breezed her way into the bar, her slim, petite figure clad from bare shoulders to toes in pale yellow silk. I had zero doubt those were real diamonds around her skinny neck and dangling from her precious little ears. As for the tiara, honestly, did she look at herself in the mirror before she left her room? Her icy blonde hair wasn't thick enough to carry off a crown, not even artfully piled in precision curls on the top of her head.

Bitter and jealous? Naw.

Personally, I thought Petunia looked better. At least, my pug would shortly. Olivia saved me the agony of the fashion show, opting for a canine version meant to pluck the heartstrings of every animal lover in attendance and hopefully create enough buzz and press to go viral online. The fact my chubby pug enjoyed her bath, manipedi and general fussing over by the staff running the show more than I did Daisy's similar attention said a lot about my own priorities.

And my pug's.

As I stood there glaring—yes, I admit, glaring was involved in my moment of weakness—Vivian's lonely singular state was the only thing that kept me from utterly abandoning my post and downing the entire bar of booze to drown my sorrows. That was, until he walked in. And ruined everything.

I'd spent so much time thinking about asking Crew Turner on a date it sometimes felt like I'd done it already and had been horribly, miserably turned down by the handsome sheriff of Curtis County. Instead, of course, out of utter lack of luck and nervousness about our present relationship's status, I hadn't. If anything, he had to be thinking I was avoiding him, dodging out of shops when he appeared, smiling like a freak and stumbling into things so I didn't have to say hello, hiding out at

Petunia's at every opportunity. All because, well, he was hot and I wasn't ready to have dinner with the man who'd once thought I'd killed Pete Wilkins.

Let's be fair here. I wasn't ready to date period. Thanks to all the trust and good will built up by my five-year relationship with my ex, Ryan Richards, ending in cheating (him) and embezzlement (him) and an attempt to pin illegal activity on me (him, strike three), I'd come to the conclusion that men and me? Not the greatest combination right now.

Didn't cut the resentment of seeing Crew pause next to Vivian looking like a movie star in his perfectly fitted tuxedo. I thought he was attractive in his uniform shirt and jeans. Yowza. Only then did I catch her blue eyes watching me, held still as she smiled and slipped one hand through his arm. And led him away.

So she'd landed him after all. Good for her. I turned to the bar for the last time, downed my drink and accepted another.

It was going to be a long, long night.

CHAPTER TWO

RATHER THAN DROWN MY sorrows in another mimosa—surely a terrible, terrible life choice that would lead to embarrassing myself and the need to vomit in public—I ordered a virgin version of tonight's ridiculously brunch-centric drink of choice and turned from the smiling bartender. Leave it to Olivia to pick something tacky.

I needed to get out of here before I "slipped" and spilled my bright red concoction down the front of Vivian's dress. Time to call Petunia's and check in.

I'd left my phone in my room by "accident." There were far too many pending air quotes in the hours that were the rest of my night, I could tell. A girl had to have her amusements. As for my phone induced forgetfulness, mostly it gave me an excuse to go upstairs and escape everyone. But after that little run in with Olivia, I second guessed my exit despite my need to be a rebel and my own woman and all that. Not because I was scared of her but because, honestly, I really did have a bad attitude about this whole thing. It was one night and I was being treated very well. If I sucked up my whining I might just manage to have a good time.

Well, there were other ways to check in that didn't require me to leave the main level. I turned and swished toward the exit of the bar and into the more brightly lit foyer, clicked from tile to pale blue gray carpet, the giant, sparkling chandelier above my head throwing rainbow light over everything, streamers and balloons shaped like hearts dangling from the huge, arching ceiling. Instead of going for rustic cabin in the woods chic, the designers of the White Valley Resort aimed for all out contemporary ice castle glamor. I personally found it a bit pretentious, far too New York for Vermont, but it wasn't my business to run.

The long, gray ash wood and glass front desk spanned the far wall, with two stations manned. I crossed toward it through the mingling crowd. A group of teens in matching snow suits giggled their way to the elevator, the lodge logo stitched on the back of their white jackets, skis and a rifle crossing beneath it. I'd heard Olivia managed to bully the owners into sponsoring a new biathlon team, among all the other things she was working on. How our mayor kept the multitude of spinning plates moving I had no idea, nor did I want to, but kudos where they were due. Though, honestly, there was something a bit desperate about chasing the new shiny too often.

Someone's elbow made solid contact with my ribs and I hissed out a warning, turning to find a young man with dark hair and that kind of handsomeness that hid arrogance and entitlement behind shark like eyes sweeping his pale amber gaze over me before winking.

"Watch where you're walking," he said. And laughed like he'd cracked the best joke ever.

He'd see how funny it was with a lap full of virgin mimosa.

"Fee?" Lucky boy, his companion distracted me, stepping around him and the small group of hangers on I hadn't noticed on my way to the desk. She hugged me around the neck with great enthusiasm while I pondered the need for the still staring young man to take up the center of the room—and attention—with his posse.

"Simone?" Recognition clicked in while Simone Alexander released me, her dark skin faintly glowing with what looked like a dusting of mica, black eyes as huge and deep as her older sister's. The youngest sibling of one of my closest friends from college, Simone had been far less put together the last time I saw her. Was that only a year ago?

"Fee!" She beamed at me, big, full lips luscious with gloss, high cheekbones accented by the stunning updo she wore, making her even taller than her normally statuesque height. She was almost as tall as her date thanks to her hair, slender body stunning inside her shimmering black gown. She clutched my free hand, her excitement in seeing me clearly genuine even if her companion came across as irritated with her distracted attention.

I kissed her cheek gently, smiling up at her. I might have been a solid 5'7"—add two inches with the heels—but Simone's six feet always made me feel tiny. Same as her sister, Jasmine, who I now missed with a painful jab of guilt. I hadn't seen Jazz since I left New York. A social worker with a gigantic heart and more caring for others than they usually deserved, she'd been one of my only friends who applauded my departure, how I dumped Ryan. She couldn't stand lawyers, though, so I never knew if she picked me for me or just to burn him. Still, I really had to call her.

"Jazz knew I was coming and made sure I found you to say hello." Simone's teeth shone against her dark skin, precise. Helped having an orthodontist mother with a thing for perfection. "It's so great to see you!"

"You, too, Simone." I glanced at her date who now pointedly ignored me, speaking to his group in a loud voice that sounded a lot like blah blah blah to me. "What are you doing in Reading?"

"Mason invited me." She tugged on his arm, hers winding through his. He turned back to me like it was no big deal while she smiled at him as if he meant something to her. So, I'd give him the benefit of the doubt for the next five seconds. "Mason Patterson, this is Fiona Fleming."

Patterson. One of Reading's founding family of Pattersons? That name registered while he spoke, making no attempt to shake my offered hand. A reflex to even extend that courtesy, but telling.

"Ah yes," he said. "You have that little motel in town, right?" Well, that was uncalled for. And clearly aimed to get a reaction. His friends laughed right on cue, low and nasty, all young, like Simone, all judging. Assholes with drinks in their hands, looking for someone to torment in their eternal boredom. Or some such idiocy. "What's it called? Pathetic's?"

More laughter while I grinned back, knowing what this was and why it was happening. Big boy here liked to show off and make himself seem more important than everyone else. I knew his type. Thing was, if he was trying to get a rise out of me, he'd just failed miserably. All the anger drained out of me, replaced by pity and I let him see it.

"Nice resort you have here," I said. "What's it feel like to be the king of small town Vermont?" I didn't wait for his response, instead patting Simone's hand while her face, now ashen and furious as she stared at Mason, turned to me with an apology behind her eyes. Forget the fury that flared in him, the way his friends looked away like they wanted to laugh at him this time.

"Pop by Petunia's before you go back to the city," I said to her as sweetly as I could. "We'll have lunch."

I walked away then, oddly recovered in the self-esteem department. Something about pegging down a pompous young wannabe made me feel so much better.

Jazz did, however, pass on her terrible taste in men to her sister. And since I wasn't much better, I couldn't judge, could I? Now my frown came back and I blamed Mason Patterson for my shift in mood. Last I'd heard, Ryan had somehow weaseled his way out of charges for the embezzling he did from his law firm, but at least the jerk was disbarred. So that was something.

"Fiona Fleming," a hand caught my elbow and turned me with precise care, my mother's face showing her disapproval. "That frown better not be something you're planning to carry around all night or I'll have to tickle it out of you." She smiled then, kissed my cheek, while I gaped at my parents, my towering, broad-shouldered dad clearly uncomfortable in his tuxedo despite how great he looked, Mom much more confident in her two-piece chocolate suit/dress that could have looked ridiculous but worked so well for her.

"What are you two doing here?" That was rude. I hugged Mom then kissed Dad's cheek while he grunted in my ear.

"Olivia," he growled in his deep voice while Mom hooked her arm through his. People needed to stop doing that. It was like a barrel of monkeys epidemic in this place, all the couples connected at the elbow. Seriously.

"Mayor Walker insisted we come," Mom gushed, her eyes my eyes, her hair my hair, though she wore her makeup and updo much more joyfully than I did. "Wasn't that nice of her? Our room has a jetted tub." She poked Dad in the ribs before winking at me. "I can't wait to renovate the bathroom, now."

Dad rolled his eyes and I laughed. Redoing the house had become an obsession with Mom since she stopped teaching and he retired from the sheriff's department. There wouldn't be a single piece of wood or even a rusty nail of the original rancher I grew up in once she was done.

"Sounds great, Lu," Dad said with false cheer while giving me that deer in the headlights look he often did these days. Poor Dad. I bet he wished he was still hunting murderers and getting shot at on a regular basis.

"Ladies and gentleman," Olivia's voice startled me over the loudspeaker, cutting through the music still playing. "The dining room is now open. Please join us for dinner."

I turned with Mom and Dad—and the rest of the guests filling the foyer—to watch the two large polished steel doors at the far end swing open. Mom clapped like a little girl going to her own birthday party while Dad looked a bit ill.

"Start with the outside forks," I told him with a grin. "You'll be fine." He just sighed. "Save me a seat." I waved to them when the mass of people moved toward the open doors with a chattering good humor that made me want to run upstairs after all. "I'll be right there."

I watched my parents go, taking a moment to admire them together. Married thirty-one years and still adorable. Okay, now I *was* depressing myself.

With a sigh of my own that I'm sure sounded a lot like Dad's, I turned and crossed to the front desk to make my call.

CHAPTER THREE

THERE WAS AN ACTUAL line at the counter and I found myself lingering at the far end of the glass top desk, considering running up to my room to save myself the wait. Except I'd find it very hard not to bring my phone back down with me and then I'd be on social media all night instead of enjoying my very special Valentine's Day dinner with my mother and father of all people.

Thank goodness Daisy's arrival stopped me because I didn't need Olivia glaring at me all night. My best friend—from high school and now all over again since my return to Reading—swept out of the elevator like an excited teenager, firmly grasping the hand of a tall, stunningly gorgeous man of northern European descent, his ice blonde hair as natural as Vivian's was fake, glossy as her ivory patent leather clutch, eyes shocking blue when they met mine while he smiled in a way that gave me shivers all the way through to the depths of my lady parts.

"Fee!" Daisy hugged me with enthusiasm before straightening my dress and then her own. She chose a short, flared skirt affair for her own gown, a delicate blue lace sweater skimming her narrow shoulders. The sapphire pendant she wore looked new and nothing like the fake ruby necklace she'd picked out for herself. Nor did it appear to be costume, about as real as the giant diamond on her companion's middle finger. "You look fantastic." She giggled before turning to her date. "Emile, this is Fiona Fleming. Fee, Emile Welter Ries."

"How could such a small town be home to so many stunning beauties?" Emile bent over my hand, kissed it with his wide lips, those amazing eyes actually twinkling. I'd seen strong jawlines and gorgeous bone structure in New York, but holy hell in a handbasket. Daisy knew how to pick them.

I stuttered a thank you while knowing I really needed to be offended or something to be looked at the way Emile looked at me except my heart was pitter-patting and my insides had found it necessary to turn to liquid fire under his gaze.

"Emile is visiting from Europe," Daisy gushed.

"Luxembourg," Emile said, smiling at her like a doting and patient boyfriend. Jealousy punched me briefly before I jerked myself under control.

"How exotic," I muttered, then winced inwardly. "You're visiting Reading...?"

He shrugged elegantly inside his tuxedo, shirt open, tie missing, though his pocket square was as blue as the sapphire around Daisy's neck. "I'm considering investing in your town," he said, flashing another smile. His voice had that cultured French lilt to it that told me he'd been born abroad but educated for a time here in the US, likely in the northeast. Harvard, possibly, or Yale. "And so far, I'm delighted and impressed with the potential for growth and opportunity."

One of Olivia's recruits. "We're happy to have you," Daisy gushed at him. "Isn't he adorbs?"

Emile laughed, a real laugh and I couldn't fault her the choice. Unlike Mason Patterson and his old money arrogance, this man—no boy in sight—had the kind of self-assured confidence and well balanced empathy that came from real wealth and centuries of tradition.

"We'd better find our seats." Daisy paused, eyebrows raised. "Are you okay?" She glanced at the desk then back to me. "Do you need anything?"

So sweet of her but I shook my head, waved them off. "Going to check in with the sisters," I said. "I'll be right there."

Daisy led Emile away, chattering on about Petunia's to him while I watched them go and wiped the drool off my chin. Okay, so exaggerating, but still. Yumtasticness had wandered into Reading and just increased the gene pool in a most delightful way. Maybe that meant my chances of finding someone weren't as dismal as I'd been thinking. Sure, I'd told myself every night the last eight months going to bed with only a farting, chubby pug for a partner I didn't need anyone. But I knew better.

Need was a strong word. I was fine on my own. Want, on the other hand?

Want had just hit an all-time high.

I turned to the desk with a little sigh of frustration only to notice someone had butted in front of me and the line was as long as ever. Grumble. Fine, whatever. Nature called, another distraction, pushing me away from the counter and the pair of barely out of their teens whining about not having enough towels in their room toward the public washroom sign on the other end of the lobby from the dining room. At least I didn't have to fight my way through a crowd this time, feeling rather obvious and self-conscious to be crossing that giant foyer by myself. Not like anyone was watching, so why did I care?

I must have taken on a bit of a confrontational strut because I reached the entry to the washroom's hallway in record time and had to pull myself under control again before I broke into hysterical giggles over how utterly ridiculous I was being. And halted, breath caught, at the sound of raised men's voices. Blame it on Dad's genes or instincts or whatever you want, but I froze and eavesdropped like I was born to it.

"—mind your own business," one said. I peeked around the corner, the doors leading to the men's and women's washrooms flanked by giant plants, two young men exiting the large, swinging door to the boy's room before standing in the middle of the hall with anger bubbling between them. The one in the waiter uniform chopped the air between them like he was done talking. "What Ava and I do isn't about you, Noah."

"Bro," the one he called Noah said, brothers or brothers in arms? No, when I caught a good look at their profiles their blood ties were pretty obvious. So that address was literal. "You're not listening to me. You need to talk to her again before you make more plans."

"I already have." The waiter brother looked sullen and frustrated. The other clearly wasn't serving staff, but he worked here from the long sleeved shirt logoed with the lodge patch over his chest and the crisp black dress pants and shoes. "Stop butting your nose where it'll get broken."

"Mason Patterson will do more than break your nose," Noah muttered.

Fury flared on his brother's face, tall body taut under his dress shirt and bow tie, narrow hips twisting beneath his long, black apron. "Ava has nothing to do with that jerk," he said.

Noah didn't respond, and that seemed to make things worse for his brother. And from what I knew of Mason, I didn't blame waiter boy for being pissed. I barely met the kid and I couldn't stand his ass.

"You're being a blind idiot," Noah snarled while his brother actually formed fists at his sides, the two leaning toward each other like blows were inevitable. I hesitated, ready to break up the fight before it happened, when a young woman came hurtling around the corner past me, brushing against me in her haste, to confront them both as if she hadn't even seen me.

"You two," she snapped, "will stop this right now or I'm kicking both of you where it hurts." She wore a similar uniform to Noah and the pair looked like they stood in solidarity against the waiter brother. Maybe not on purpose, but he slumped, sullenness returned, face grim and still angry. He stalked off without another word while she called after him. "Ethan!"

Noah grabbed her arm, stopped her from pursuing him. "Just let him cool off. I'm going to throw on my tux. You go change into that fancy dress of yours before we're fired for being late to dinner."

She tsked at him before hurrying past. Only then did Noah notice me, eyes widening, eyebrows raised, embarrassment warring with clear guilt.

"Sorry about that, ma'am," he said, stepping back and gesturing at the bathroom door. "Enjoy your evening." And then he turned and followed the young woman—the very Ava from the Perry's conversation, I assumed—and disappeared.

I should have been the apologetic one, but if management caught the staff fighting in front of guests, well. I'd worked enough service jobs to know who'd get blamed for being the guilty party. I noted the out of order sign on the men's door and wondered if the brothers had been looking for privacy and put it there to keep others out. Well, they hadn't done a very good job, had they?

A quick refresh and I was back to business, though the last thing I was expecting when I hustled out the bathroom door was to almost impact with a hulking man in dark blue work clothes who glared at me on the way by, the out of order sign dangling from one big hand. A large tattoo across his neck that appeared to continue under his dark hair as if he'd been taken to shaving his head at one point gave me the creeps. For which I immediately kicked myself.

Judging by looks alone? I knew better. And yet, that glare of his wasn't exactly friendly and I'd encountered enough animosity in the big city to know when to stay out of someone's way.

Whatever and none of my business. Focused on one more try to reach my own staff instead of policing someone else's before Olivia personally dragged me in to my seat like an errant child, I headed for the front desk and a phone.

CHAPTER FOUR

I EXHALED IN RELIEF at the sight of the empty lobby. The desk, now cleared of other guests, stood waiting for me, though the single person behind it made me wonder what kind of reception I'd get. Surely the staff was overrun with all the crazy Reading residents by now? Sick to death of us? From what I'd heard, the bulk of the employees here had been hired out of town, something Olivia had to answer to the council for. But her plan to increase prosperity and lower the unemployment rate meant the lodge had little choice, so anyone complaining was doing so to hear the sound of their own voice.

Despite my worry about her attitude, the young woman on the other side smiled at me with that kind of expression all front desk people perfected so you never knew if they were actually interested or just doing their job.

"Can I help you?" She sounded cheerful and professional enough, dark brown eyes fixed on me, bottle blonde hair in a neat bun at the base of her neck. The light was harsh here, showed the faintest blemish scars hiding under her makeup but she smiled like she meant it when I leaned over the counter with a big eye roll.

"Might I use your phone?" I set my drink aside. "Just a quick call, local?"

She nodded immediately, passed over a handset while keying the pad to an open line before offering it to me to dial. I did quickly, not even thinking about the number anymore. One more bit of proof I'd fallen into the kind of life that would never, ever let me go.

"Sorry to keep you waiting," she said as I leaned into the handset that rang and rang with no answer. Had I dialed the right number after all?

"No problem," I said, hanging up and trying again. "I run a B&B in town, so I'm in an acutely sympathetic line of work."

She beamed at me then, relaxing a little. "How lovely. I've always wanted to run a bed and breakfast."

I grinned back, though the ringing phone was making me nervous. "Same problems, smaller scale. And no one to pass them off to. Well, darn." I hung up again, frowning at the phone. "No answer."

"You're calling home?" She didn't move to take the phone away.

"Petunia's," I said, nodding. "The very same B&B. The ladies looking after it are older. I worry."

She seemed genuinely concerned. "Did you want me to keep trying?" She glanced at the front doors to the lodge, hesitated. "I'm not sure what time you arrived?"

"Lunch time," I said. Daisy's idea. Make a day of it, she said. It'll be fun, she said. Before she dolled me up and abandoned me for dashingly delicious.

"Well, the weather has taken a turn," she said, sounding worried herself. "A storm's come up, unexpectedly." She looked at the doors again, clearly nervous. "They're saying the plows are being pulled off the road."

I grunted in surprise. So the weather girl had been right after all? Who knew that could happen? "Good thing we have rooms," I said. Not that a bit of snow bothered me, but I genuinely wanted to go home and make sure the ladies were okay. Now that I wasn't moping around with my head up my butt, I took a moment to look out the glass entry into the darkness and realized the girl was right. Snow swirled in giant twisters around the bright lights, though I knew from experience it often looked worse than it was.

Still.

I turned back to find the front desk girl with a remote control switching the large monitor screen on the wall behind her to the weather channel. There was attractive young brunette, Morgan Fischer, with a perky smile and a pink sweater pointed at a green screen projection behind her while a giant blob of white smothered our area of the Green Mountains.

"—severe winter storm advisory," she was saying like she was announcing a sunny day, "has been issued for Curtis County with the center of the storm focused on the Reading area."

Of course it was.

"—this low pressure system just came out of nowhere." She tossed her hands and laughed like this was funny. "Though, I did predict snow, so don't send me emails that I didn't warn you!" She giggled though it came across as a little bitter. I wouldn't have wanted her job. "Now dig in, Curtis County. You're in for a bit of a going over by good old Jack Frost. Back to you, Bob and Amy."

Just freaking lovely.

Front desk girl switched the image back to the looped footage of young people swooping through fresh powder, the ad for the lodge making even me want to ski and I hated it, before returning her attention to me. "I'm so sorry," she said, looking flustered and worried, staring down at her screen. "There's an excellent chance we'll lose our power and I have a lot of work to do just in case. If you'll excuse me?"

"Happy Valentine's Day," I said, saluting her with my drink. As I realized I needed to switch back to alcohol. Because there was a very good chance, like it or not, I was stuck here for real now. Any illusions I had about escaping in the wee hours and going home before Olivia could stop me were shattered by the betrayal of Mother Nature.

She tried a sympathetic smile as she glanced up at me before going back to work. I really should have just left her alone. Worry that Mary and Betty were right now in need and I was at a stupid ass Reading rah-rah party when I should have been at Petunia's drove me to try the phone one more time.

Finally, on the fifth ring, right when I was ready to hang up and risk heading for town—Olivia or no Olivia—the phone clicked and a five-pack-a-day voice said, "Petunia's."

"Mary." I almost laughed in relief. "Is everything okay?"

"Fine, Fiona," she said. "We keep losing power, flickering on and off the last hour. And the phones are acting up." Even as she spoke, the line crackled.

"I'm going to come home." Our dear mayor could just deal with it.

But Mary's heaved sigh cut me off. "Not sure what it's like up the mountain, but I can't even see the street outside," she said. "We're hunkering down for the night. Guests are happy, everyone's okay. We have the generator if the power dies completely." I could almost see her rounded shoulders rise and fall in a fatalistic shrug. "You stay put and safe, Fiona. We'll see you when this blows over." And then she hung up on me. Or the line died. But the former was much more likely the case.

Why did being trapped here feel like about the worst fate ever? Because I now had to walk into the full dining room by myself, date free, and sit with my parents on Valentine's Day like the loser I was.

I replaced the handset carefully so I didn't smash it down and tossed back the last of my virgin mimosa. At risk of embarrassment and public puking, it was definitely time for something stronger.

I was halfway to the doors when Olivia's voice hounded me the rest of the way in like a sheepish child who'd done her wrong.

"Dinner begins in one minute. One minute! All guests, please take your seats."

Because being bossy was an art form, I guess. But the best part? By the time I reached the big doors— with two young men in uniforms waiting for me to enter with smirks on their faces—I was the last person aside from staff still standing. The. Last. Person. That meant, as the doors behind me swung shut, trapping all of us in the vast room dissected down the center by a long, ruffled runway and flanked by layers of equally long and lavishly decorated tables, it was about as obvious as a walk of shame while I did my best not to bow my head or speed my steps toward—get this—the front of the far table where my parents chose to plant themselves.

Forcing me to walk the longest ever distance in the history of long distances while being stared at by the entire guest list not to mention the glaring smile/grimace of our dear mayor waiting at the podium on the riser that served as her stage and the entry of the runway.

Yup. Fiona Fleming. Miss Awkward 2017.

I slipped in next to Mom and exhaled, reaching for the tall glass of bubbling liquid in the flute in front of my plate. Champagne wasn't my favorite, mimosa or no mimosa, but I gulped it down in two long swigs while Olivia fired up her vocal chords and got this crap show underway.

CHAPTER FIVE

"THANK YOU ALL FOR coming to the celebration of our town and the opening of this most spectacular venue." The room applauded politely while I blocked her out and stole Mom's champagne to follow mine. By the time Olivia was done prattling on about how gracious the hosts were to have us and how amazing our town was and oh, wasn't this just the best year ever and don't forget to vote in the election to keep her as mayor, I was feeling a bit buzzed and much more relaxed than ten minutes ago.

Dad grinned at me and saluted with his own glass but Mom squeezed my hand while I exhaled my bubbly breath and leaned in.

"Slow down or I'll make you eat bread," she said. Blah. Moms.

A handsome older man in a white tux coat and a red rose in his lapel joined Olivia on stage, a taller man behind him, hook nose clearly broken at some point in his life, his own tuxedo carefully crafted as evidence the injury hadn't held him back from making lots and lots of money. I hiccupped delicately—Mom's scowl telling me I wasn't as ladylike as I thought I was—and listened as Olivia introduced them.

"Lucas Day and James Adler, our kind hosts, ladies and gentlemen, and the owners of our very own White Valley Ski Lodge."

"And Golf Club," the white-jacketed man said with a smile.

Olivia beamed. "Of course, Lucas. Opening this spring."

More polite applause. I burped softly and looked around for more to drink, Mom's shoe pointedly getting my attention. Dad seemed to be enjoying himself immensely. I crossed my arms over my chest, the pushup bra Daisy made me wear digging into my breastbone and under my armpits. The discomfort triggered irritation and I scowled at Mom for being a killjoy.

Getting drunk and passing out seemed an excellent option despite my earlier reticence.

"I think you're forgetting who really owns this place." My head jerked around, eyes locking on Mason Patterson seated down the table across from me. Simone sat next to him, hissing in his ear, looking embarrassed, but Mason seemed cruelly amused. Lucas scowled while the young man went on, Olivia's blistering stare doing nothing to silence him. "Mummy dearest died and left her fortune to me, remember?" He stood, wobbly on his feet, waving his arms around him like he owned the place. Which, I guess, he did. "And as the singular representative here tonight of the entirety of the Patterson family—because no one else could be bothered to come, Olivia, how do you like that?— I'm wondering when you're going to shut up." He tossed back a glass of his own, triggering a bit of squeamishness in my stomach I might evolve into that big a jerk with enough alcohol. "Where's *my* speech?"

"Oh, do sit down, Mason." I hadn't seen Aundrea Wilkins, nor her partner Pamela Shard, until now.

"You're not the only Patterson here and you know it." They also sat across from me, though the daughter of that founding family with her blonde hair and pinched expression didn't seem all that happy to be there. I knew how she felt. The singular newspaper woman of our little town nodded to me while keeping one hand on her lover's back.

"And you mind your own business, Auntie Andy," Mason said, vicious in his amusement. "Maybe your little lesbo lover could gag you for us. I'm sure you'd adore that."

I gaped at him, buzz gone, paling out in utter shock. Oh, but he wasn't done, was he? Not by a long shot. He was just winding up, I could see it on his face, in the way he filled his lungs to continue his tirade. Except, bless her, Olivia Walker wasn't about to let some young upstart—big money or no big money—ruin her perfect event.

"Shall we welcome our very special guests," she said far too loudly, gesturing with a hasty hand at the back of the room until music hastily boomed out of the speakers flanking the stage, silencing the weaving and clearly inebriated Mason who fish lipped a moment before falling into his seat. "The charming fashionistas of Reading, Vermont!"

The curtain parted and, with her tongue lolling out and a perky pink tutu bouncing around her waist, Petunia emerged in the lead of the pack. Why was I not surprised she took front row center? They'd somehow managed to make her leave the costume be and not tear it off herself, her pink painted toenails matching the giant sparkly heart hanging from the glittering collar they'd fastened around her neck. She moved at a sedate pace, waddling her way toward the end of the runway where a young woman knelt with a handful of what had to be treats in her hand.

Considering the unfaithful creature would do anything for food, I wasn't too hurt by her enthusiasm. Still, she was my pug, or I was her human, or however that relationship was going to be classified down the road. But despite my jealousy over a dog, I couldn't resist her cuteness or the fact that she clearly won the hearts of the crowd with her rolling, drunken sailor walk with her butt end scooting out sideways as if trying to go its own way and her bug eyed adorableness.

I wasn't a fan or anything.

Next out was Cookie, the petite little fluff of nothing and silence that Aundrea and Pamela adopted when Peggy Munroe went to prison for murdering Pete Wilkins. I'd been horrified to find out the reason for the little dog's silence had nothing to do with training and everything to do with the fact the wretched old woman had Cookie's vocal chords removed. One more reason to hate her. And made me just as happy my nosey neighbor and real life sociopathic criminal mastermind was gone. No more poking her nose into my business. Or organized crime, that I knew of. And I didn't have to murder her for abusing the dear little creature who bobbed happily down the aisle toward Petunia.

Cookie had clearly gone to a good home because both of her new moms beamed as the tiny tot of a canine bounced her way down the runway in a wobbling bow and dragging a skirt she'd already shed from her tiny body. She nearly ran into Petunia's butt as the pug sank to her haunches and begged for more treats while the line of Reading's most adorable dogs just kept coming to the sound of utter delight from the crowd.

By the time the last pooch—a very well trained black labradoodle named Ralphie—tugged on a rope and exposed a "Thank you for coming!" sign, the crowd's mood had lightened and everyone was laughing, even Mason, Olivia's fashion show a clear hit. Not to mention the handful of dogs who clearly didn't get the memo about where they were supposed to walk and what they were meant to do during the show, now wandering among the guests licking legs and looking for crumbs.

The young woman who'd encouraged the entourage of pets carried Petunia to me and deposited her at my feet with a beaming smile, her cheeks rosy from the effort. "She was the star of the show, Fee. Thank you."

I grinned at Lily Myers, Reading's favorite groomer and trainer and reached down to pat Petunia's wrinkled head. "If only she'd be this well behaved at home," I said.

"Free lessons for my girl." Lily blew Petunia a kiss before clicking and giving her a treat. I let her go without comment, staring down at the pug who licked her chops and looked back up at me with longing. "Room or stay for dinner?"

Like she was willingly going anywhere. Because the waiters, now circulating, brought salad and Petunia didn't turn up her nose at anything.

I was fairly certain she wasn't supposed to stay, the bulk of the dogs vanishing with the staff, but my pug girl was smart enough to stay tucked under the table, accepting morsels from Mom and me, content to sit on her wide pug butt with her back legs poking forward and her eyes never leaving us. Even Dad got into the act, tossing her the occasional tidbit as dinner went on.

Olivia arranged entertainment, a parade of young people singing pop songs and a creepy guy who did a few magic tricks before she shooed him off stage in favor of a couple who ballroom danced down the runway. But the real show of the evening was the rapidly devolving temper of the young man across the way. The more he drank, the worse Mason became and while I couldn't make out most of what he was saying, it was clear from the occasional swear word and jabbed finger at other guests accompanied by laughter while Simone looked more and more like she was going to crawl under the table, he was as big a jerk as my first impression told me.

"Someone needs to handle that boy." Mom's disapproval mirrored mine.

"No one has the balls." Dad grunted when she poked him in the ribs for being rude. "It's true."

"You don't have to be vulgar about it, Johnathan Fleming," she said with a sniff.

I grinned at him behind her back, mouthed, *Sucker.*

He stuck his tongue out at me. "Yes, dear."

She made a face, frustration clear. "Go say something, would you?"

But Dad shook his head, focusing on his drink. Likely a double whiskey on those rocks he rattled in response, his favorite. "Not me," he said with a grin. "That would be Crew Turner's job."

Mom tsked at him before her eyes roved the room and I instantly felt sorry for the new sheriff if he didn't get up right now and do something because if Mom had to go ask, he'd regret it.

Instead of letting Crew suffer my mother's wrath, I changed the subject. "How's your dinner, Mom?" The beef seemed a bit dry to me, but the potatoes were delicious.

She tried a smile before poking her own meat with her fork. "Honestly, how can anyone treat a prime rib this horrendously and get away with it?" So that's why she was really upset. Not about Mason Patterson after all. The truth came out the second she was given permission to complain about the food. "And these vegetables. Were they boiled until they were tasteless on purpose?"

Mom's amazing culinary abilities had always held me in awe considering that was something I hadn't inherited. I might have looked like Lucy Fleming with her auburn hair and green eyes, but I had my father's soul. I never knew if that made Mom sad or not, but I certainly wished at times it was the other way around. At least then I could cook a decent meal while not holding an old grudge against Dad for ensuring I didn't go to the police academy in his footsteps.

Protective sheriff fathers sucked sometimes.

"I really shouldn't go on." Mom touched her lips with her napkin, leaning back. "I know Carol and she's lovely. But her food just isn't up to snuff." She glanced over her shoulder, face tightening. "I wonder if that's the kitchen."

I smothered a snort of hilarity and sipped more sedately at the refreshed glass of champagne a nice young waiter gave me. No more need to drown my sorrows, not when I had the entertainment of John and Lucy Fleming to keep me amused and distracted. And I'd been worried about dinner with my parents on Valentine's Day. Sitting there with Petunia now squatting on my feet with her warm butt, I couldn't think of a better way to spend the most miserable night of the year.

Movement across the table caught my attention. Mason was leaning over Simone and talking loudly with a young woman on her other side. I recognized her then as Ava, the girl from the bathroom hallway, spotting Noah on Mason's other side looking uncomfortable but staying silent. Ava, on the other hand, seemed incredibly unhappy and Simone just glared between them as if she was ready to murder them both.

How fun.

The ballroom dancing couple wrapped up as slices of chocolate tower cake emerged from the kitchen doors in the hands of the fast moving servers. I couldn't miss the piece that settled before Mason, noted it was Ethan who delivered it, glaring at Ava all the while. Someone put a big, blue candle in the middle of Mason's slice, the tiny flame flickering. He laughed and blew it out, tossing it aside before taking a big bite of cake. With his bare hand. He offered the dessert smeared fingers to Simone who looked away, furious.

I glanced away, attention caught by talented Ralphie the labradoodle—Lily's dog, naturally—who performed his final trick with precise precision. Tail wagging, a big tux collar and bow tie bobbing around his shining, fluffy black neck, he trotted down the runway and tugged one last ribbon. This time, instead of a sign, the net overhead parted and a soft, quiet fall of red heart balloons tumbled toward the crowd in slow motion.

The gasps of delight turned to popping sounds as guests reached for and burst the balloons, some with treats inside. Punctuated a moment later by a long, powerful scream.

I leaped out of my seat, staring across the runway to where Simone stood over Mason, her mouth open in a perfect circle, that piercing sound emerging, silencing everyone, while the young Patterson sat motionless, face first in his chocolate cake.

CHAPTER SIX

MY INSTINCTS GOT ME moving, but I couldn't just hop over the table in my short dress and heels. I found myself pursuing my father who had the exact same genes if years more experience with stuff like this. He did the work for me, making a path when people tried to stand up, creating a trail I could follow down to the end of the table and up the runway to the fallen Mason and still screaming Simone.

Crew had appeared out of nowhere, beating us to the scene, so he had to have been sitting further down my table and out of view. Clearly I'd missed seeing him out of sheer stubbornness and focus to get to my seat not so long ago. Must have blocked Vivian out, too, thankfully.

It was apparent from his expression as he straightened from touching the young man's neck there was nothing he could do. His blue eyes met mine just before he jerked his chin at Simone, a clear request—I wouldn't accept order—in that gesture before he spun and leaped over the table, one shoe landing firmly in the middle of the white table cloth in the exact place nothing sat. Like some kind of action hero. He made it to the stage area and had his hands on the microphone before even Olivia could pull herself together.

I slipped under the table instead of risking people seeing up my skirt by trying Crew's cross over method and emerged to hug Simone and silence her as the sheriff's voice crackled through the din of chatter that had broken out, music abruptly cut off as whoever ran the audio shut it down.

"Ladies and gentlemen!" When Olivia said it, it sounded politico. When Crew said it? Everyone shut the hell up. Impressive. I patted Simone's back, half turning her away from the body, foot slipping on something as I shoved her chair back out of the way. I looked down, Petunia at my feet, the pug sniffing a small, shiny object on the carpet. "Please remain calm." Funny how cops always said that when terrible things happened in large groups of people. Seemed to work though. I released Simone long enough to retrieve the thing I'd slipped on, stopping myself at the last second and using a discarded napkin to pick up what looked like a glass vial right before my greedy pug could swallow it. "If you would take your seats for the time being and allow me to do my job, I would appreciate your cooperation."

I hugged Simone again, tucking her against me while she shook and wept. Dad's big hand settled on my shoulder and I looked up into his eyes, his own narrowed and his face unhappy.

"Bring her here, Fee." He guided us out of the way, Mom appearing to hug my friend's sister, too. Simone collapsed into the chair my mother offered her, Mom perching next to her and rocking her while I stared down into the napkin in my hand and tried to sort out what just happened.

Crew appeared at my side, but his eyes were on the body. "I need help." He sounded like that hurt, asking. Dad joined us and nodded. "I need to get people back to their rooms so I can examine the crime scene." He grimaced, turned to both of us, looking harried and worried. "I tried calling the station."

"There's a storm," I blurted. Dad looked surprised then grim. "The plows are off the roads."

"Now you tell me." The sheriff didn't sound accusatory, just tense. Good thing, too. Because the storm was not my fault, thank you very much, Crew Turner. "That's why I need your help. But this is my investigation." He spoke directly to Dad. No, wait. He was talking to me, too. Well, considering I'd done a bit of poking around into Pete Wilkins's death and not only uncovered the prescription drug theft ring his sister was orchestrating and the falsification of signatures that meant the theft of local properties but also single handedly brought down his murderer.

Well, with Petunia's help. But she had paws, so she didn't count as "handed." And maybe "little bit of poking around" was an understatement, but that was neither here nor there.

"At least the weather means the killer isn't going anywhere either." Dad said that like he hadn't heard Crew just tell him to be subordinate.

The sheriff nodded. "We have that in our court," he said, the "we" kind of warming me up to the idea of playing nice. "But no forensics, no fingerprinting, nothing. Just us." He swore softly under his breath while my mind told me not to suggest any street wise, down and dirty forensic measures I'd seen on my favorite police procedural shows, knowing how much Dad made fun of what Hollywood chose to present as possible to move a plot along. "And no doctor, either." Crew's jaw jumped.

"Where's Walter?" Dad looked around.

"Dr. Aberstock is in Florida for his daughter's wedding." Olivia joined us like she had been standing there all along and was actually in charge of this particular conversation. "He was unable to change his plans." That sounded like she tried hard to make him miss his own kid's nuptials. That was our mayor. Class all the way. "You three." She swallowed and squared herself. "I need you to get this sorted out." For the first time since I'd met her Olivia looked harried. Out of control. Well, fair enough. Though murder hadn't seemed to bother her when it was Pete Wilkins on my property and my watch. No fun when the tables were turned. "I will not have my event ruined by this inconvenience."

Wow. She did not just call Mason Patterson's death an inconvenience. Even she seemed shocked by her words. We all stared at each other a long moment of utter surprise before Olivia simply spun and marched away, joining the understandably agitated pair of Lucas Day and James Adler.

"At least her priorities are always clear," Crew said. Dad chuckled then cleared his throat like this wasn't a laughing matter and he knew it.

"What do you need, Crew?" Dad sounded sympathetic enough and Crew, after a second of squinting at the carbon copy of himself with three decades added on, nodded with a soft relenting of tension.

"Get those who we know aren't remotely involved in Mason's life back to their rooms in an orderly fashion."

Dad nodded. "We can ask the staff to help," he said, raising his eyebrows at me. "Fee, too?"

Crew met my gaze, his as close to pleading as I'd ever seen. "Yes, please. While I talk to the girlfriend."

"Wait," I said, putting two and two together and coming up with something unpleasant. "You think it's murder? For all we know, he died of alcohol poisoning. Or he had an aneurism. Or a heart attack." My fingers clenched around the little vial I'd found under Simone's chair, catching Crew's attention. He grasped my hand before I could stop him, pulling my wrist until I opened my hand and revealed the vial. An oily smear had formed on the napkin, the familiar scent of peanuts drifting up from it while Crew's teeth made that grinding sound and the vein on his forehead appeared and pulsed like it had been waiting for me to do something he didn't like.

Before he could say anything, I handed it to him. "I found it there," I said, pointing. Knowing it didn't look good. "Just now, as a matter of fact, so don't be a bully about it." Yeah, he loved that accusation. Then he shouldn't be manhandling me, should he? "But it's just peanut oil or something."

Simone's gasp behind me echoed from the handful of young people who stood around, watching the horror unfold. And I knew then that Crew's instincts were right and that I was only trying to find alternatives to Mason's passing because of my friend's sister. And the fact it was very likely the murder weapon sat in the napkin in the sheriff's hand.

"Mason," Simone whispered. "He was allergic to peanuts."

The young man from the fight outside the

bathroom spoke up, eyes meeting mine, recognition flaring there.

He nodded grimly. "Anaphylactic," Noah said.

CHAPTER SEVEN

I INSTANTLY MOVED TO protect Simone, knowing what came next out of experience. I'd been the focus of police attention not so long ago and my protective nature reacted before I could stop myself. Not that I would have, though. I caught the flash of anger in Crew's eyes but ignored it because she was my friend's little sister and no way was I going to tell Jasmine Alexander, Amazon queen of fiery tempers and dramatic orations—not to mention utter loyalty to the death—I let her baby sis be questioned for murder without doing my best to keep her safe.

Crew didn't argue despite his attitude, allowing me to stand there and hold Simone's hand with Mom still supporting her on the other side while he focused his attention on the still weeping young woman.

I have to say, however, the hideously frustrated and furious look on Vivian French's watching face? Worth it. Even murder. Yes, I was that petty, knowing from how her face scrunched despite the work she'd had done just how Crew asking me for help had to be devouring her insides like a rabid squirrel. Thoughts like that kept me warm at night. Though it was likely a certain Sheriff Turner wasn't in for so hot a reception when Vivian got him alone again.

Petty, Fee. And distracted. So much so I almost missed Crew's initial volley at Simone.

"You knew he was allergic," Crew said. Winced because dumb question, Sheriff. So he was far more rattled than I'd originally thought. He held stiff and still, purposely not looking at Dad who hid a grin behind one hand. "Obviously."

Simone sniffed and nodded, too upset to notice or care. "We all did." She waved her hand at the crowd of young people in their pretty dresses and identical hair and tuxedos. Cutout copies of Mason Patterson, one and all. His posse bobbed their heads like puppets cut free of his strings, a bit wobbly but in full agreement. While one of them might be the killer, I didn't see a whole lot of light in their eyes or originality either, so part of me dismissed the lot of them. All, that was, but the girl Ava who stood to one side with her arms crossed over her chest, the tall Noah beside her, both hands in his pants pockets, scowling and not looking as sad as maybe he could have.

Distraction from my line of thought appeared in the person of Lucas Day. He pushed his way through the semicircle, his face blotchy and eyes bulging with what could only be grief, a smear of something on the lapel of his white jacket which he seemed ignorant of in the moment.

Chocolate, looked like.

"What happened?" I'd seen his kind of daze before, the blank overwhelm of sorrow and stunned confusion that took over when someone died. Dad had it a little when I arrived home after Grandmother Iris passed. And Mom when her own parents were killed in a car accident when I was a teenager. It looked as if someone struck him on the back of the head, though it was shock from the death rather than a blow of the physical kind that made his knees wobble and his hands shake. At least, that was my guess.

The cynic in me studied him more carefully than the empath. For all I knew he was drunk or stoned or something, though he didn't give me that impression earlier, and I quickly shoved that side of me down deep and agreed to feel guilty about the whole dive into suspicion. At least for now.

While Lucas might have been sober and suffering, his partner, on the other hand, wove like a consummate alcoholic through the gathering, the telltale signs of frequent imbibing starting to show in the broken capillaries on his cheeks and the polished way James Adler carried himself despite the drink still clutched in one hand. And, unlike his partner, he seemed less than upset by what just happened. The booze, maybe? Or maybe not.

"He died," James said, saluting Mason's still prone body. So, not just the booze, then. Something else, something triggering the kind of heartless reaction that maybe drove a man like him to drink in the first place? Crew hadn't even pulled Mason's face out of the cake yet. I knew why, the necessity of preserving evidence, but it seemed rather heartless considering the look on Lucas's face, the way Simone glanced at her dead boyfriend over and over again. Mind you, Mason wasn't really a nice guy to begin with, so the irony of him dying in so much sweetness wasn't lost on me.

I left Dad and pushed past the kid posse as Lucas spun on his partner, rage replacing shock. "Shut up, James," he snapped before returning his attention to Crew. I shoved aside glasses and plates and a red rose centerpiece, freeing a section of tablecloth while Lucas's voice carried to me despite the noise I made. "Tell me what happened. Mason was in perfect health. This was not death by natural causes."

The sheriff held his ground and I had to admit I rather appreciated his total calm and cool composure in the face of the distraught father as I returned with my makeshift corpse covering. "We have no solid cause of death at this time," he said, nodding to me when I held up the tablecloth and pointed at Mason. I slipped between him and Lucas and draped the sheet over the fallen young man when Crew continued. "Without the proper testing and forensic analysis, we can only guess." I twitched the cloth one last time, tucking the corner over Mason's hand before turning back to catch Crew scowling at Lucas who opened his mouth to interrupt. "I don't guess, Mr. Day. Ever. Now, you're the victim's father?"

"Stepfather," James interjected, a hint of humor in his voice, in the twist of his mouth. "Mason old chap there was Marie Patterson's son from her first husband. He kicked the bucket out of sheer desperation to escape the old bitch, isn't that right, Lucas? Then you went and married her and it was her turn to croak." He laughed, a bitter bark that made me flinch and caught Crew's attention. Though oddly Lucas didn't defend himself. I let that go because he stood, eyes down, staring at the floor, hands shaking. Stepson or not, he'd lost his wife and now the young Mason. It had to be devastating no matter their obviously troubled relationship.

Still, people killed other people for really dumb reasons. And Mason was a jerk.

"John and Fee." Crew nodded to us, and I realized then I was about to be cut off from the investigation. From the deep scowl on Dad's face, he made the same connection in that moment. "Please proceed with emptying the room as we discussed. I'll handle this."

He had to be kidding. He had multiple suspects lurking around. From the sound of things everyone in his life knew Mason was allergic to peanuts. Anyone could have used that against him. Crew needed us to keep an eye on the others while he questioned each individually.

Dad had made the same assumption. "Can I talk to you, Sheriff?"

Crew looked like he already knew what my father was going to say and yet he stepped away and joined us like he was going to war. Brave, but stupid.

"I don't have time to argue with you, John," Crew said.

"Or to spend hours interrogating a single suspect," Dad said. "I know your methods, Crew. You need to be fast on this."

"I don't need you to tell me how to do my job." And there it was, the bitterness between them, the pushback of testosterone that got Dad's back up, too.

"Have you ever been in a situation like this one, kid?" Oh, Dad. You called Crew kid, really? I knew immediately it was a huge mistake.

"Have you?" Nice back challenge, but as it turned out, Dad nodded.

"Hunting lodge, 1984. I was a deputy then and one of the hunters was murdered. We were stuck up the mountain. I learned fast that day, Crew. Almost lost the killer in my need to be thorough when speed was more important."

"Well, we'll just have to disagree there," Crew shot back, though I saw the doubt in his eyes. "I trust my training, my experience and my techniques. And now, if you will please do as you said you'd do and help me, I need this room cleared and the guests secured in their rooms."

All those years of instinct and wisdom staring him in the face and here he was, Captain Do-It-All, sending away the only two people in the room who could actually help him.

To my shock, Dad didn't argue. At all. Instead, he nodded to Mom before grasping my arm and tugging me away from Crew and the body, the suspects, Simone. All of it. I hissed at him when I managed to find the energy through my shock to protest, jerking my arm free even as Dad spoke in a low, tense voice.

"I'm going to do some looking around," he said, "while Crew is occupied with his endless interrogations. Your mother knows enough from being married to me all these years to keep your young friend from saying anything that will incriminate her." He grimaced. "As for you." Dad met my eyes and I realized there was sadness there. "Fiona, I can't believe I'm going to say this, but you do what you do best. Go poke your nose in where it's not wanted. That fool," he jabbed the air in Crew's direction, "doesn't understand how our minds work or just what he's up against with a lodge full of suspects and no trust for those he could use to his advantage." Dad just said "our." Did he really just say "our?" "He just gave us the freedom to solve this case while he's bogged down with the endless procedure he's dragged here with him from California."

Yeah, no resentment there or anything? And yet, as I glanced back at Crew, the covered body, the gathering of people doing as he told them for the most part, I decided to give the new sheriff the benefit of the doubt. "Or," I said, relaxing out of my instinctual kneejerk to being sent away, "he knows exactly how we think and that's why we're out here and he's in there." Dad joined me in watching Crew, surrounded and alone, taking the full weight of the visible investigation on his shoulders, arguing with James and Lucas while Mom hugged Simone.

I looked down as something warm settled on my feet and sighed. Petunia followed me and I'd forgotten all about her. I had to tuck her into my room at some point or give her over to Lily to take care of. For now, she could follow me while I did my best to do what Crew asked—and what he didn't— and maybe uncover something that might help.

"Dad." I grabbed his hand, squeezed it as he turned to go. "Thank you. For trusting me."

He squeezed back. "I wish I'd done it a long time ago. But you showed me in July I was wrong all along, Fee. And I'm sorry. Maybe it's time to look at the police academy. If you still want to go."

He left me then, staring after him in stunned silence, chest pounding, unable to breathe for a second. When air finally filled my lungs again I shook off the shock and followed him, my mind turning over what he said.

CHAPTER EIGHT

NO MATTER HOW I tried to focus on the task at hand, guiding people out of the dining room in small groups and to the elevator, my pug offering licks for those who bent to pet her, while Dad organized them in tidy, orderly fashion no one questioned thanks to his casually commanding air, I struggled to forget what he'd said. Could I really think about giving up my life as it had evolved for a chance at being a cop like him? At my age? Of course I could. But did I want to? The idea appealed, as always. The thing that didn't? Starting out as a rookie at what would amount to thirty or thirty-one if I was going to be honest about it. Not so appetizing. I'd just had my twenty-ninth birthday in October. And while the lifelong dream lingered thanks to our conversation, I felt old as I led yet another cluster of nervous guests across the foyer and saw them safely away with my best B&B owner's voice and the charm I learned from Mom, Petunia's cheerful panting and grunting adding that extra layer of all was well to the point the entire experience felt more surreal than solid.

As the room slowly emptied, guests following Dad's directions and my clicking heels better than I'd expected, I wound my mind around becoming a police officer for real, at last. And, when I turned in the end to the mostly empty dining space, I sighed and shook my head to myself.

Maybe, had I the chance at eighteen. But no. Petunia's was my fate, the B&B and the pug, at least for now. I was happy in my new home, happier than I ever expected to be. Solving mysteries, hunting down murderers and criminals of other kinds while appealing in a romantic sense, well. I knew what thinking about a job like that in those terms meant. Delusion, disappointment and probably death at the other end of a criminal's gun for being so stupid to think I had what it took.

"Fiona." I caught my breath, hand coming to my chest in shock at the interruption. Petunia chuffed a greeting, warm rear on my feet when I stopped and turned to find Malcolm Murray, the owner of The Orange pub, standing behind me, smiling at me. The old Irishman nodded in greeting, bending to pat Petunia who accepted his greeting with her normal pug grace. His longish gray hair fell over his forehead, those green eyes as piercing as mine meeting my gaze when he straightened once more. While his wrinkled face told his age, he had a lean dangerousness to him, his eyes at my height as he saluted me with his glass. Looked like whiskey, same stuff Dad drank. And here was a criminal who my father knew well, who had an arrangement with him when Dad was sheriff. At least, as far as I knew.

"Malcolm." He'd visited Petunia's a few times for tea over the last few months, making small talk with the ladies and being a perfect gentleman. I'd even sat with him once, poked and prodded a bit for info, but he was a wily sort and I'd only ended up with a cute story from his days as a boy in Ireland, a mention of Grandmother Iris's fine cooking and frustration.

I'd refrained from telling Dad about the visits because his initial reaction to me informing him I'd met Malcolm was shock and horror. Despite the fact the Irishman spoke highly of Dad.

Interesting and a puzzle for another time, but one I'd been neglecting long enough. I might not have wanted to pursue a life of police work, but that didn't keep my curiosity from stirring.

"Sad state of affairs, murder," Malcolm said, taking a sip from his glass. "The young man might have been a butthole and a gobshite but no one deserves that fate."

I loved the lilting accent and had to shake myself from the mesmerizing cadence of it, despite the swears.

"Who said it's murder?" I grinned to soften the challenge and Malcolm laughed.

"You and your da are involved," he said. "That's enough for me, my Fiona lass."

I missed his approach, should have expected it, shocked still when Dad interrupted us by storming to a stomping halt next to Malcolm, towering over the slim Irishman and firmly planting himself between me and The Orange's owner.

"Fee," Dad ground between clenched teeth, shoulders stiff. "If you're done sorting guests, go help your mother."

Well, that was a dismissal if ever I experienced one. And while I would have loved to argue—oh, would I—I also needed to make sure Simone was okay. This whole mystery around Malcolm wasn't going anywhere.

"Nice seeing you again," I smiled at the bar owner who chuckled wickedly in approval of my obvious jab at Dad. I might have been leaving, but he'd better not think I was going because he told me to.

"Fee. Thanks for the chat, lassie."

I walked away, glancing back as subtly as I could but might as well have not bothered trying for subterfuge. The two talked with bent heads, Dad looming over Malcolm who seemed totally at ease despite their size difference. Whatever it was they had between them I'd find out sooner or later. And it was clearly personal or Dad wouldn't be so worked up, would he?

Maybe Mom would know.

Speak of the devil, Petunia hustled ahead of me to sit beside my mother, looking up at her with, I realized, hope in her puggy eyes someone—namely Mom—might feed her. Since my darling mother was such a terrible source of food the portly canine loved and I regretted thanks to the flatulence such treats usually created, she was Petunia's first choice for begging.

Which made me wonder if my mother secretly laughed at me, knowing exactly what she was doing. I wouldn't put it past her.

Mom patted the pug's head to Petunia's disappointment before meeting my eyes with her worried ones. The small group of copycat young people stood off to one side, Crew talking to them, Lucas now collapsed in a chair a few feet away, James beside him, still drinking, a bottle next to him on the table. Someone had finally pulled Mason out of the cake, the body sitting mostly upright, still covered in the tablecloth I freed for that use. The plate of cake had been secured inside a big plastic bag, likely liberated from the kitchen. I wondered if Crew had stopped to clean the chocolate from the victim's face. Or if Mason Patterson sat under that sheet with his handsome good looks smeared in the dessert that killed him. At least there wouldn't be any exterior signs of the attack, so when his father put him in a casket, he'd still be pretty.

Maybe that was a sick line of thought, but I came by it honestly. So I studied this stuff in my free time.

And had since I was a teenager. Was that so wrong for the daughter of a county sheriff?

Rather than go right to Simone, I had some questions for Lucas, knowing Crew was going to be a while before he talked to Mason's stepfather if Dad's assessment was accurate. I was in the mood for some poking my nose in where it wasn't welcome. With a steady sympathetic expression, I sat next to the older man, offering him some fresh water from the pitcher on the table. He accepted with a nod, still dazed, while my eyes skimmed the chocolate smear on his jacket.

Could have come from anywhere. And yet... chocolate and peanut oil made a killer combination. Mason was pretty drunk. Would he have missed the scent of the oil in his inebriated state? Seemed obvious the answer was yes. Unless the oil ended up in another source, it had to be the cake. His death just happened too fast otherwise, the three minute timeline my research into anaphylaxis's most severe attacks said was a perfect fit for the moments between him eating the dessert by hand and Simone screaming after the fall of the balloons masked Mason's struggle with his reaction and collapse. No wonder no one saw him dying. Bad timing.

Or the killer's intention? That and the vial of oil definitely made the case for murder.

"Mr. Day," I said, keeping my tone compassionate and low, "my deepest sympathies for your loss. It can't be easy to lose both your wife and your stepson in such a short time."

"Thank you." He sipped the water. "Miss?"

"Fiona Fleming. I'm assisting Sheriff Turner in the case along with my father, John Fleming?" I left it at that when Lucas nodded. Good, so he knew dad was sheriff before Crew. And wasn't questioning my involvement further. "Can you tell me what Mason meant? About the ownership of the resort?"

Lucas swallowed hard while James let out another of those bitter laughs.

"Tell the girl, partner," he said, resentment bubbling under his alcoholic haze. "Tell her how Marie fronted the bulk of the project so she could control it. Tell her how between us we had 49% and she had 51%. That when she died that monster she raised and the family she adored got everything and you got *nothing.*" James sagged in his seat, staring into his drink like he'd lost the will and the strength to be angry anymore. "Tell her that with Marie's death we lost control of the business we built together and that

Mason and the damned Patterson family were going to kick us to the curb."

"They couldn't do that," Lucas said, sounding like he almost meant it.

"Oh, they could." James shrugged, a dramatic rise and fall of narrow tuxedo shoulders. "The Patterson family can do anything they want in this town, can't they?"

"They were going to buy you out?" I prodded Lucas gently, but my choice of words were aimed at his drunk partner.

James shook his head, lifting his drink to his lips before pausing. "Shoving us out," he said. "Controlling the brand, undermining our power until we're both just here for the free booze. And offering us pennies per share to cut and run."

Sounded like motive for murder.

"Mr. Day," I said. "With Mason gone, who has control of the resort?"

"The Patterson family," Lucas said, eyes dull and voice cracking.

So not motive, unless straight up revenge for a deal gone wrong. But I just didn't buy that, not from Lucas. Maybe from James, but still. As far as I could tell at this point, Mason's death meant nothing for these two men. Or was a downhill slide into further worries. "I'm so sorry," I said.

"Miss Fleming," Lucas said, cleared his throat, his shock slowly wearing off as he pulled himself together enough to meet my eyes without that wild kind of look one gets in moments like this. "While Mason and I had our differences," James snorted but stayed silent otherwise, "he was still my stepson and I raised him from when he was a boy. I cared about him and I would never kill him. Not only was he my only connection to Marie," he said her name like he actually loved her still despite the impression James gave me of her, "and killing him would gain me nothing financially."

"I understand," I said, glancing at the partner who smirked and saluted with his whiskey. "And you, Mr. Adler?"

James winked at me, hand wobbling, sloshing the ice in his glass. "I'm glad the kid's dead," he said. "But dying screwed us further. So you decide if that's sufficient motive for murder."

He downed the last of his drink before reaching for the bottle. Lucas stared at his partner for a long moment before shaking his head as if making a choice not to speak further and instead sank deeper into his chair, gaze locked on the floor.

CHAPTER NINE

I WAS ABOUT TO rise and leave Lucas to his mourning when I noticed a few familiar faces on the other side of the room. Aundrea Wilkins waved to me, Pamela beside her, Jared Wilkins and his girlfriend, Alicia Conway, lingering close by. I'd had the occasional encounter with the four of them over the last eight months since Pete died, and always pleasant. In fact, my eyes drifted to the giant diamond on Alicia's hand, the very one she'd been delighted to show me just a week ago when she showed up at Petunia's to tell me Jared finally proposed. I was happy for them, that they had found each other despite his father's crimes. And that Jared seemed to have avoided any legal issues thanks to his willingness to assist authorities to correct his father's mistakes.

I joined them while Dad took my spot, Malcolm now nowhere to be seen, Petunia huffing her way along with me at the last minute when she realized Mom wasn't going to be forthcoming with food any time soon. And took advantage of the pats and greetings her appearance generated while I rolled my eyes and sighed.

"Fiona," Aundrea said, hugging me quickly before Pamela did the same. There was no sign of Cookie so Lily must have taken her away or the ladies stashed the little dog in their room. I really had to do the same with my pug before too long. She was totally under foot. Make that on top of foot as she sat on my toes like always with a grunt and a soft, happy fart of warm air that heated my skin and made me cringe.

"I'm sorry about your loss, Aundrea," I said. "Mason was your nephew?"

She snorted and crossed her arms over her chest, the glitter of crystals sewn into the top of her deep pink gown catching the light from the chandeliers overhead. "It might make me a suspect in your eyes, Fiona, but there was no love lost, trust me. And if you're going to make a list of possible murderers out of the people who didn't like him, you're going to be here a long time."

"Did Crew rule it murder?" That sounded pathetic, and like a feint.

"Come on," Pamela said, the news woman in her showing, sharp eyes skimming the scene before her. I loved that she wore a tuxedo and wished I'd had the guts to do the same. No, the idea. Next event, I was pants and jacketing it all the way. "Everyone knew he was allergic to peanuts. The kid almost died a few times because of them so Marie made a huge deal about it to make sure the entire town knew." And provided the means for his demise. Not his mother's intention, I imagine. "No way this was an accident. Which means someone purposely gave him what would kill him."

Right. "So, anything you can tell me that might help?"

"I might have something." Jared joined the conversation, nodding to me, Alicia nervous at his side. While I'd been accused of killing his father, Jared held no grudges and, in fact, helped me out, releasing Petunia's back to me without a fight when Pete tried to use a fake signature to claim my dying grandmother signed it over to the developer. Jared could have fought it and might have won—would have bankrupted me with lawyer fees at the very least in the battle—but instead, as he did with everyone else Pete wronged, he did everything he could to make sure all the victims of his father's schemes were compensated for the frauds outside the help he gave the police and FBI.

"You knew Mason?" They were a bit off age, Jared at least five years older.

"I did," Alicia said, glancing up at her fiancé with those big eyes and that worried expression, shifting in the long, slim wrap of gold crepe she wore, draped elegantly over one shoulder. Nice to see her wardrobe had leveled up since she stopped having to wear the slutty suits Pete insisted on. "He wasn't a good person, Fee."

"Yeah, I'm getting that," I said. "But?"

"It's James Adler," Jared said, voice dropping. "If anyone, I'd pick him."

"Why?" Since I'd just talked to James, I had my own suspicions. But if he had another motive outside financial, that would be helpful.

"You were still in New York when it happened," Jared said. "His daughter, Elizabeth, disappeared and is presumed dead. Skiing accident in Aspen."

James's last comment just a moment ago and the way Lucas reacted... but surely he'd known I was going to find out. Or that Dad knew, or Crew would uncover the truth? Why not just tell me he had a second motive? Because while Jared hadn't finished, I put two and two together and got a big giant reason to kill the young Patterson. "Let me guess," I said, skin tingling with anticipation. "She was with Mason."

"James blames him for her loss," Alicia said. "But no body was ever found and there was no proof he hurt her, so..."

And that, ladies and gentlemen, was a solid motive for murder if ever I heard one.

I left them with instructions to go to their rooms before Crew spotted them and gave them a hard time. With the exception of Aundrea, that was. She made her way to Lucas and crouched at his side to talk to him. She, at least, was a kind soul despite her Patterson breeding. Maybe she could help.

As for what I'd uncovered, I needed to talk to Crew. And joined him just as the young woman

Mason had been hitting on—the same one from the fight in the bathroom corridor—was speaking.

"Definitely died from anaphylaxis," she said, her gaze flickering to me a moment before returning to Crew. Maybe Dad was wrong about the sheriff's speed. He seemed to be working the scene far more quickly than my father said he would. Someone had spread the body out on the stage with the sheet still intact, dark brown seeping through in the lump area that was Mason's face. I looked away, caught Crew frowning at me but he didn't send me away, just gestured for Ava to go on.

"Ava Hiller, this is Fiona Fleming."

"Nice to meet you," she murmured.

"Ava is premed," Crew said, "and her father is a doctor."

So, best he could do under the circumstances. "You've seen this before, Ava?"

"I have, in fact," she said. "I was just telling the sheriff. I actually saved Mason from this very situation in college last year. His birthday. Someone brought a cake but didn't know, I guess, had put peanuts in it. Mason just ate it, too drunk to notice." She seemed frustrated by that before shrugging. "I happened to recognize the signs and was able to use my injector in time."

"You have allergies?" I asked that very question the same instant Crew did and won a scowl from him for interfering. Tongue between my teeth I did my best not to be sent away while Ava nodded.

"Shellfish," she said. "I carry one with me all the time."

"Why didn't Mason have one?" Crew looked down at the notepad in his hand. It had the lodge logo on it, as did his pen. He was making the best of a bad situation. And had he taken Dad's suggestion to heart? We'd see.

"He never cared enough to carry one." That was from the waiter, Ethan. I hadn't noticed he'd come to join the posse of whispering young people who comforted each other while snagging drinks from the tables around them. Classy. Ethan interjected like he was angry. "Thought he was invincible even though the idiot almost died. If it wasn't for Ava, he'd have been long gone."

The loyal crowd gasped and muttered, but Crew ignored them.

"And you are?" The sheriff honed in while I waited for him to answer.

"Ethan Perry," the waiter said, sullen and suddenly acting like he wished he'd kept his mouth shut.

"And you know Mason how?" At least Crew was asking the same questions I would. Saved me from being noticed.

"We went to college together," Ethan said. Turned to scowl at the posse. "We all did."

And yet, he was a waiter and the others were in tuxedos and gowns, including his own brother. Noah stood with the group of young people, sneaking someone's abandoned champagne. So why was Ethan relegated to slinging plates when the others looked like they were part of the It crowd?

Crew seemed curious about the same thing. "Did you, by chance, deliver Mason's dessert tonight?"

I hadn't made that connection and tsked to myself even as I recalled seeing that very thing, mind flickering to the image of Ethan delivering the towering cake with the flickering blue candle. My protest at my own failure emerged loudly enough Crew noticed but didn't comment.

Ethan, on the other hand, paled before nodding. "I did," he said. "But I didn't kill him. I had no reason to."

Ava grasped his hand, her own expression anxious. "Ethan would never," she said. "We were all friends and have been for two years. Mason invited us to come and work for him here at the lodge. We're all employees." She gestured at the group. "I'm a ski instructor, Ethan's brother, Noah, is a snowboarder. The rest work in other areas that had the night off. All but Ethan."

"Pretty glamourous," Crew said. "But you're a waiter?" He stared pointedly at Ethan.

The young man's face tightened, whole body tensing. "What's wrong with waiting tables?"

"Nothing," Crew said. "As long as being the only one working on a night when everyone else is partying isn't some kind of punishment Mason handed out."

Ethan didn't comment while I recalled the conversation between Noah and his brother. About Mason and Ava. And how Mason had been obnoxiously ignoring his date—my Simone—to talk to the pretty ski instructor.

The way Ethan looked at her, the conversation with his brother, all fit a relationship between them. But, before I could bring it up, Crew closed his note pad and nodded to them.

"I'll have more questions later," he said, grasping my elbow and leading me away before I could do my own investigation. "I need you to go to your room now," he said, "and stay out of this."

"You were the one who said you needed help," I shot back, keeping my voice low as we approached Mom and Simone, Dad beside them. "I'm not leaving now."

"If you stay," he said, voice vibrating with intensity, "you keep your mouth shut and observe only. I'm not kidding, Fee. And you tell me everything you find out."

I opened my mouth, tons to share, only to have him walk away from me. Because being a jerk had to be on his long list of faults, didn't it? How was I supposed to tell him what I knew if he wasn't going to listen?

Frustrated and ready to wash my hands of all of it, go to my room with Petunia—who still trailed after me looking for food—and watch bad TV, empty the minibar and wish him luck. Instead, anger bubbling, I followed him if only to make sure he didn't somehow decide Simone was guilty.

CHAPTER TEN

S HE WAS CRYING AGAIN by the time I joined them, Crew already at her, obviously. And looking like he was settling in for the long haul too, planting his butt in a chair and crossing one shiny dress shoe over his knee, pad and pen in his lap. If only he didn't look so fantastic I could muster some angst against him and feel more like a defender instead of a participant in her questioning. At least I had the satisfaction of accepting he hadn't learned from what Dad said. So be it.

"I swear, I didn't kill him." I knew how Simone felt. I'd been in her place, though I hadn't done any crying. Probably because I'd secretly—and horribly—been relieved Pete Wilkins was dead in my koi pond.

That the man who tried to steal Petunia's from me had kicked the proverbial bucket before he could do any more damage than he already had. And, a further note that separated my experience from Simone's was the fact I hadn't been dating the person who so abruptly died.

Um, wow. I really didn't need that visual of me and Pete Wilkins on a date, thanks. Ew and more ew and oh my god what seed of horror had I planted to come out and give me nightmares later? Grossed out by my own imagination, I hung back, hugging myself while Crew spoke.

"You've never seen this before?" He produced the small vial with a clear skim of oil inside, still cradled in the cloth I'd used to retrieve it. Yeah, Crew. Me. *My* clue. Well, Petunia's if credit was going where it was due. I was gratified I seemed to have preserved the evidence as well as possible considering he still used the same napkin to protect it.

"No, I haven't." Simone shook her head with great emphasis, shining crown of hair immobile despite the vigorous gesture. Whereas I'd done almost nothing so far and I felt like Daisy's well placed pins were letting go, giving up the ghost in the battle against the massiveness that was my hair. I absently rubbed at a spot that was starting to ache from the pressure as she looked up with those huge, dark eyes and bit her lower lip. "Is that what killed him?"

"Peanut oil," Crew said, tucking it back into his jacket pocket. "Drizzled on his cake." He'd either confirmed that by a sniff test before tucking the dessert into the baggie now resting next to the body or was assuming. Considering I didn't get the impression Crew made assumptions when it came to crime scene investigation, I had to think the former. Now who was guessing? "You were sitting next to him when his dessert was delivered?"

"Yes, all evening," Simone said, snuffling while she wiped at her tears. She still looked stunning, like her sister did the few times I'd seen Jazz weep, able to cry and not get that just sobbed her heart out look. Unlike me and my Irish heritage and all the blotchy hideousness that came with a good, solid cry. Instead, she seemed vulnerable and lovely and there was no way she murdered Mason. Not biased or anything. "I can't deny he was being a total dick. But he was a nice guy under all the swagger, I swear. Until he started drinking." She looked down, clasping her hands around a used napkin in her lap, mascara and remains of lipstick staining it in spots. "I hated it when he drank."

"Tell us what happened," Crew said, sounding at least a bit sympathetic, though knowing him he was just softening his tone to keep her talking. And talking. I'd stay until he started repeating his questions and move on. Since she wasn't saying anything incriminating and Dad wasn't trying to shut her up—Mom either—I let things progress.

"He was being so mean to everyone tonight, saying horrible things." She glanced up at me, gestured in my direction. "Even Fee, and that was well before dinner." Crew glanced at me with that of course I was involved in more ways than one look before turning back to her. Apparently Mason wasn't the only jerk in attendance tonight. "And then he started hitting on *her* like he always does."

Wow, where did that shift in direction come from? Simone's anger appeared at last, Jazz's self-righteous fury all over again. One did not try to muscle in on the Alexander women for fear of the kind of vocal retribution that could cut like a weapon apparently. Well now. Was I mistaken about my friend's little sister, far too much like Jazz for her own good? I'd seen firsthand just how far she'd go to get back at a cheating partner's new girl. Watched said new girl dissolve into a puddle of apologetic sobbing while the guy begged forgiveness as Jazz walked away, victorious. A symphony of holy crap what just happened to watch. But did Simone's temper lean more to murder?

Oh, Fee, don't be like that.

Simone's fingers tightened on the napkin, the fabric so tight I was sure she'd tear it as she went on, anger fading into hurt. "I just wished he didn't have to do it in front of me all the time."

"He had a thing for Ava?" Crew sat forward, voice prodding Simone who stared at the young woman in question across the room like she blamed her for everything.

"Ever since Ava saved him at the party last year," Simone said. "He's been obsessed with her. But Ava and Ethan have been together since high school. She's always turned Mason down."

Didn't keep her from sounding bitter about it.

"How long have you and Mason been dating?" Crew scratched a few words on his notepad, leaning back again. Definitely settling in for a nice, long session. I hoped Simone's anger would show up at some point and give him a ride.

"A month," Simone said. "He's been really lovely all along. Until tonight."

Good at hiding who he really was, I suppose. "Simone," I said, "you must have known he wasn't who you thought. If you were friends for so long, you saw the truth of how he acted."

She shrugged, tried a little smile. "You sound like Jasmine," she said. "But I saw good in him, too, Fee. And when he asked, how could I turn him down? Everyone wanted to date Mason, even if it always ended in heartbreak."

Well, you couldn't argue against money and looks and a short stint of whirlwind romance. Or could you?

"Simone, where's Mason's injector pen?" Crew's question caught her off guard and she jerked upright.

"Here!" She tugged open her bag, presented it to him. "I used it as soon as I realized what was happening." Her hand shook, the pen dropping from her fingers. He was fast enough to catch it before it hit the floor while she hugged her purse to her chest. "It all just went so quickly. I thought he was messing around, being a clown. When I finally realized he was dying, that it wasn't a joke…" She shuddered and more tears fell, a long inhale necessary for her to speak again. "I used it, I swear. But it didn't help him and I don't know why."

"Empty." Crew examined it another moment before tucking it into his jacket. "Did it dispense?"

"I have no idea." She sagged again, Mom patting her shoulder. "I've never used one before so I didn't know what to expect. But I tried." And then she dissolved into weeping again while Crew sighed and looked down at his notes, clearly ready to start all over again.

The exact moment the room went utterly dark.

CHAPTER ELEVEN

SOMEONE SCREAMED WHEN THE power went out, red beacons flashing into existence as emergency lights flared to life in response to the loss of electricity. I stumbled over Petunia, looking down to find her glistening eyes appearing as my vision adjusted.

"Everyone stay calm." Dad's voice carried, followed by Crew's.

"Please remain where you are until your eyesight acclimates," the sheriff said, sounding exactly like my father. "The storm may have knocked out the power." He turned to me. "Fee, can you go check and see when the generators will kick in? Otherwise we need an alternate source of light."

I nodded, bending to scoop Petunia into my arms and hurried toward the doors. At least the space was easy to navigate even in the dark, the tables in an orderly layout that left me a clear path to the exit. I was just passing through the big doors when I almost ran right into Olivia.

I'd never seen panic in her eyes before. "We have to do something," she said. "This is a disaster, Fiona!" Her pale dress appeared ghastly in the reddish glow, horror movie worthy, olive skin demonic. Didn't help how her eyes bulged like that.

"It'll be fine," I said in my most soothing tone, depositing my chubby pug into her arms. Petunia licked Olivia's face, the mayor snuggling my dog in a way that told me she'd needed a bit of comfort and realigned my thinking about our dear leader. Anyone who Petunia liked—and who liked her back—was a good person at heart. "Come with me, we'll see if the generators are working."

The girl behind the desk wasn't around, leaving me frustrated and leading a nervous Olivia Walker behind me while she rhythmically patted the pug over and over again. I had a fear of heights so I could only imagine the mayor's reaction was something similar, possibly a phobia of the dark. I slipped around the counter and peeked into the back but no one was around. Just a heavy coat with snow still on the collar and a pair of winter boots dripping on the carpet. Someone had been outside. To check the generators? No, the snow was already melting. The owner of the coat couldn't have been that fast.

I turned and squeaked in nervousness to find Olivia followed me, both her and Petunia staring with bugging eyes, the red emergency lights reinforcing her demon appearance, only now my pug looked possessed, too. At that moment, the lights flickered overhead and came back on, though dim enough at first to tell me the power hadn't been restored but that the generators were working at least.

Olivia instantly transformed, clearing her throat, handing me Petunia. And grasped my elbow in a claw like grip. "You tell no one of what you've just seen," she said.

"Nothing to tell," I said.

The mayor straightened her dress, squared her shoulders and marched out of the office, leaving me with a bemused Petunia and my own amusement. I set the pug on the floor and went to the desk, the farting creature following me with her nose to the ground in case there were precious snacks she might uncover. I let her scrounge, hoping the worst she could snuffle up wouldn't hurt her, finding it weird to be on the other side of the counter looking out. A quick check of the phone line gave me dead air and the TV behind me showed static, the satellite feed out. I was pretty sure if I made it upstairs and checked my phone I'd have trouble with cell reception, too.

Stupid storm. Worst timing ever.

I bent to lift Petunia again, her hunt unsuccessful, and froze, the sound of a door opening and closing at the other side of the office catching my attention.

"I'm telling you," a man's deep, guttural voice said, obviously continuing a conversation he'd started before entering the room, "one of the snowmobiles is missing from the shed. We should tell that sheriff it's been stolen."

"I doubt it's stolen." I didn't know that voice and peeked inside. A woman in a black suit with a nametag looked harried, her short, red hair spiked as if she'd been running her hands through it. Management? "And the sheriff has enough to worry about, Bill. Just leave it for now. One of those damned kids probably borrowed it and left it out in the snow."

He grunted, towering over her, the man from the bathroom hallway in the maintenance clothing. He looked up, caught me watching, and gestured. The woman turned toward me while he retreated. She spun when he left her, calling after him.

"Just keep those generators running!" She twirled back, smile on her face, hand extended toward me. "Employees only, ma'am. You'll have to go now."

"Fiona Fleming," I said. "I'm assisting with the investigation. You are?"

She hesitated before continuing her attempt to guide me out of the staff room. "Donna Walker, general manager. Now, if you'll excuse me?"

I found myself out from behind the counter and her bustling off, my pug in my arms and a missing snowmobile on my mind. I crossed back to the dining room and the continuing questioning of Simone. Confirmation that Crew hadn't listened and that he was hell bent on following his own procedure no matter how silly it seemed under the circumstances.

Oh well, who was I to judge? For all I knew his endless questioning and generally irritating behavior might drive the killer around the bend so far they had to confess just to get him to shut up. Sure, right, that was logical. Not.

I pondered my next steps, gaze falling on the posse seated across the room, Dad observing them. They were in line, I guess, to see Crew. Had my father questioned them already or was he waiting to see what the new sheriff would do? I loved my dad but was he above letting Crew dig himself an embarrassing hole just to prove a point? Um, Fleming. Right.

"Mom." I turned to her, Petunia sagging in my grip, way past her nap time.

"Don't say another word." She held out her arms, far enough from Crew and Simone we had privacy but close enough I knew my friend wasn't alone, not really. The sheriff might have asked my mother to step away, but her eagle eyes were locked on my friend and there was no way she'd let him bully Simone past her limits. "Go see what your father's uncovered." She caught me staring—okay, glowering—at Crew and Simone and reached out to take my hand. I looked down, feeling my stiffness as a reaction to my protective nature ease a little under the weight of her calm, green gaze. "She'll be all right, Fee," Mom said.

She'd better be. I left my mother with the grunting, farting creature, feeding her bits off someone's dinner plate, and made a straight line to Ava name who stood hugging herself, her off-the-rack black dress no match for Simone's sparkly attire. Yet, the young woman had nothing of deceit in her as she stared at the now draped body of her friend, Mason, laid out on the stage with a tablecloth covering him.

"You saved his life, you said." I jumped in without preamble. "Used your own injection pen to do it."

She shrugged at me, turning away from the lump that had been Mason Patterson. "I didn't think, just acted. My dad's a doctor and I've wanted to be one since I was a kid. At least, until recently, I thought I did." She cleared her throat before turning her pretty hazel eyes on me. "It was one of those instinctual things, you know? I saw him choking, turning blue, knew what was happening—I'd had it happen to me and knew the symptoms—and just jabbed him." She mimicked the action with one fist, up and then plunging down like she was stabbing herself in the thigh. The intense look on her face gave me a moment of worry before she shook her head and tossed her hands.

"You were friends at the time you saved him?" I wasn't doubting her sincerity, but her boyfriend's unhappiness was tied to this so I needed to dig deeper.

Ava shrugged halfheartedly. "Not really. Mason always had girls hanging around him but mostly he was friends with Noah and, through him, Ethan. It was the first time he seemed to notice me." She glanced sideways at Ethan and I put some things together.

"And after that he noticed?" She nodded while I went on. "And Ethan noticed him noticing." Another nod, a faint smile. "Was Mason's attention welcome?"

She shook her head this time, but sadly. "I wasn't into him, not at all." That sounded authentic and so was the shudder of disgust on her face. "Mason wasn't my type."

"What, you're not into handsome, rich guys who are utter dicks to everyone around them?" We shared a little laugh at that, though she instantly looked guilty. "It's okay," I said. "I have a feeling Mason would be laughing with us before firing off his own volley."

She grinned, then relaxed. "He had his occasional good moments," she said, as if trying too hard to speak kindly of him before she sighed. "And his incredibly cruel ones." She bit her lower lip then leaned closer, whispering. "Ethan should be teaching skiing, not Noah. He's twice the athlete and a better instructor and Mason knew it."

"But when you all showed up for jobs at the lodge?" It wasn't hard to figure out what happened to the guy who was dating the girl Mason wanted. Not when that same guy was in a waiter uniform and his rival under a sheet.

"He gave Noah the teaching gig and made Ethan wear an apron." She didn't sound happy telling me this, but it didn't stop her. "And we had no choice by then. We all sold our stuff and gave up our apartments and our second semester of college this term because Mason made us such a great offer. And he honored every promise."

"Except the one he made to Ethan." I'd be pissed off. Not only did the asshole shaft him the job he promised, Mason was hitting on Ethan's girlfriend on a regular basis.

Ava's face twisted like she fought tears. "Something like that."

"Ava." I already knew she wasn't guilty, but I had to ask anyway, though Crew likely had. "You were one person from Mason, only Simone between the two of you. Why didn't you use your injector pen again?"

She looked like I'd stabbed her in the heart. "I didn't notice what happened until it was too late," she said, choking on tears that spilled from her big, hazel eyes. "I swear, I would have. And I should have had time." I nodded. Three minutes or so. A mystery we might not get an answer to until the autopsy. "Simone was leaning in, trying to keep him from talking to me. She's so much taller, she blocked my view. And then she was shaking him and screaming and it was too late." Tears welled, her lashes blinking against them, voice thickening in genuine regret. "I'm so sorry. I would have, I honestly would. It's a horrible way to die."

I hugged her, feeling terribly for her, but believing her. And even more inclined toward Ethan than ever.

CHAPTER TWELVE

I GUIDED AVA TO the bathroom and left her there to clean herself up. She had nothing to do with the murder, I was certain of that. Why save a guy a year ago only to kill him now, especially when she had zero reason to and others far more motive? Like her boyfriend, case in point. Well, he needed a good digging into. Which led me to the left of the hallway instead of the right, down the corridor toward the kitchen rather than returning to the lobby.

The big, swinging door with the round window revealed stainless steel and appliances on the other side. I had the right place. Should have brought Mom with me, she would have loved a peek at the big, industrial space with tall ceilings and massive banks of ovens on one wall, a real brick pizza oven in one corner, cooler doors at the far end and long, metal tables with racks overhead for prep dividing it into sections. I'd done enough waitering myself over the years I could identify the breakdown and headed toward the very back and the office door there.

I found Carol Chaney in her office, the space crowded with boxes of goods and piled with invoices. She sat with her head in her hands, tiny and silent and so still I wondered if she'd fallen asleep. Her staff had gone, nowhere to be found, obviously sent to their rooms. Dad was doing a better job than me following Crew's orders. Or more likely had his own plan of attack for the investigation and was clearing those he thought unconnected to the crime.

She looked up as I knocked, pale brown eyes red and bloodshot, her tinted hair obvious from the thin, new line of white at the roots of her dark blonde. The head chef surged to her feet, her name clear on her badge so I knew I had the right person, and glared at me while she hitched a breath past her continuing tears.

"The kitchen's closed," she said, voice gruff, deep and belying her petite body, her vulnerable trembling.

"Fiona Fleming," I said, "working with Sheriff Turner and former Sheriff Fleming while we wait for the deputies to arrive." She relented when I finished, sinking back into her seat. "Can I ask you some questions, Chef?"

She tossed her scarred and muscular hands. Not a big woman by any means, like most people in her profession she had powerful fingers and palms, covered in old knife cuts and burns from the perils of her job. "I don't know what else I can tell you," she said. "Your father was already here." She frowned. "Told me it was my cake that killed Mason. Something about peanuts." The chef seemed almost offended by that. "As if I'm inexperienced enough to allow such contamination in my kitchen." She sagged then, shook her head. "He was very thorough."

As I suspected. Though, like Crew, Dad had a rougher side to him that might not get him what he needed. Instead of diving into asking her personal questions, I started elsewhere, letting her see my empathy as I spoke. "I'm looking for Ethan Perry."

She squinted up at me, trust building slowly. Why, because she put things together and thought I suspected him and that she was off the hook? Better for her to think she was helping me find the killer instead of defending herself. "One of the waiters? I don't know where he is. Why?"

"So you don't know him very well?" Her answer could go one of two ways, depending. Some chefs made it their mission to know everyone in their establishment intimately. Others treated them like the help. Her response would tell me what kind of boss Carol was.

"No," she said. "But not for lack of trying." Door number one, then. "The kid has a giant chip on his shoulder that no one's been able to shift." I wondered why. Sarcasm. "Do you think he had something to do with this?"

"I'm wondering if you keep peanut oil in the kitchen." Carol's face stilled and she seemed hesitant. I stepped aside as she stood then, nodding, wiping at her nose with her black sleeve, heading for the main cooking area. She scooped up a matching bandana, tying it around her bob, as if resuming the full uniform of her profession gave her strength. For all I knew, being Chef gave her superpowers. Though, Mom didn't seem to think that applied to her cooking skills.

Bad Fee. Stay focused.

"Of course," Carol said, pulling me back from my wandering thought tangent that had her dressed in tights and a cape instead of her black coat and bandana. "I stock it, but I've never used it. Not after Lucas told me about Mason's allergy. And honestly I've been cutting it out of recipes for years because of the trend toward nut issues. I only keep it for specific requests and it's never allowed out unsupervised." Like the bottle itself was an errant child requiring babysitting. She stopped at a tall cupboard, pulling it open. Crowded spices nonetheless had a kind of order I sorted through mentally as she shifted a few things around before grunting softly and leaning away. "It's not here."

Da-da-da-dunnnn.

Hands shaking, she turned to me. "I always keep it in a plastic bag to ensure it doesn't touch anything else. But the bag and bottle are gone. I have no idea for how long." Obviously upset by her loss, she turned to stare into the cupboard as if the oil would reappear out of nowhere.

"Carol, did you make tonight's dessert, or was that a staff effort?" I glanced over at the serving area where a few cakes and slices still remained.

Reminded me I didn't get to eat mine. Fee, chocolate at a time like this? Well, actually, yeah.

"I did," she said, voice lowering. "I know that makes me look guilty."

"Actually," I said, "we think the peanut oil was added after Mason's piece was cut. I noticed he had a candle but no one else did?"

Carol went to the dessert counter and leaned against it, staring down at her cakes with a lost and forlorn expression. "His father—Lucas—it was his idea. Mason missed his birthday last week and Lucas wanted to make an effort."

Creating the perfect signal for the killer to use for identifying the right dessert. But there was something else here to prod her about, now that I had a modicum of her trust. "You say Lucas like you know him well?" The way she flinched confirmed my suspicions.

"We... we've been seeing each other since Marie died." Of course they had.

"So Mason's father, your boyfriend, asked you to single out a slice of cake and make it very obvious it was Mason's. Is that correct?" I didn't mean to sound so harsh and softened the words at the end with a touch to her shoulder. "Could Lucas be responsible?" I'd already ruled him out, but between the two of them, could they have made this work? Or even Lucas and Ethan...

Carol's quick sob stopped me. "They had their differences," she said, "but Lucas was trying so hard. For the sake of the lodge. And because he really, really cared about the boy he remembered when he and Marie first met. Couldn't let go of that boy, actually." She sounded like she disagreed with such a choice. "Gave that kid more chances than anyone deserved."

"Did Mason know about your relationship with Lucas?" Not that it mattered. My mind spun, tried to sort all the relationships, a task quickly giving me a headache. Or maybe it was the champagne residuals from earlier.

"He did. And he didn't like it. But there wasn't anything Mason could do, short of firing me." She paused. "Before you ask, no. It was never brought up. If Mason intended to cut me loose because of his stepfather I never heard about it."

"Mason's control of the lodge had to rankle." I stuck a finger in the icing of the nearest slice and was surprised when Carol copied me with her own piece.

We took turns devouring chunks of cake and chocolate buttercream while we spoke.

"The thing is," Carol said, "he didn't have full control. If Lucas and James had just worked together, I know they could have figured it out. Yes, Mason and those horrible Pattersons were at 51%." She grunted then, stabbing her index finger into the soft and moist delicousness. "They didn't even have the courtesy to show up, did you know that? Of course you do." She shook her head. "They let Mason be their mouthpiece."

"And Aundrea," I said.

Carol didn't comment on the widowed Mrs. Wilkins. "My point is, the other forty-nine is a huge power to fight against. But James has been so absorbed by his daughter's disappearance. I'm not blaming him. Elizabeth's death hit him hard, hit Lucas hard too, knowing how James blamed Mason. But he's been distracted since she was declared dead last year and Lucas has been fighting the family alone." She sadly licked one finger clean of crumbs. "If James doesn't step up now that Mason is gone, the Patterson family will push them both out in a matter of months. And this place has been their dream for so long I can't imagine either of them—or their friendship—recovering from the loss."

CHAPTER THIRTEEN

I ATE THE LAST bite of the piece of cake I hadn't intended to ingest, thinking as I did. "Carol," I said at last, the two of us lost in silence for a long time, so long when I finally broke that quiet we both jumped a little. "I know you cut Mason's piece. But where were you when he died?" I had to ask, surely she understood that.

She nodded to me, grim. "You know already, Fiona. He was one of the first to receive his dessert thanks to Lucas. So I was here, in the kitchen, of course. Cutting more cake for the servers."

"Isn't that a job for a less experienced staffer?" She was the head chef and surely had other tasks to complete.

"Lucas asked me to make sure Mason's birthday was acknowledged," she said. "And everything was under control so I took the dessert station." Mom would have disagreed with that. Carol gasped then, eyes huge, one hand pressed to her black chef coat, fingers dark with chocolate. "I might not have killed him, but I was part of his murder, wasn't I?"

"You had no way of knowing the murderer would single out his cake," I said, feeling terribly for her but thinking the exact same thing I'd been accusing her of mentally all along, sad to see she'd just made the connection.

She sagged, face falling, faint jowls showing despite her slender features and lines pulling at the corners of her mouth aging her while her skin paled out. I grasped her upper arm to make sure she didn't keel over on me while she shook her head, hand now over her mouth.

"I might as well have painted a target on his back," she said in a voice so choked and hoarse I could barely make her out. "That candle told his killer exactly what piece of cake to dose."

I let her have her moment while my head whirled and demanded I keep pressing for answers. But my compassion won. Instead of pushing on, I stood there and held her arm and waited for her shaking to subside, her retreat into guilt making her knees wobbly. When she finally looked up again, tears streamed down her cheeks.

"Lucas will never forgive me," she said.

"You didn't do anything wrong," I told her in as firm a tone as I could manage. "In fact, you only did exactly what he asked you to do." Which meant these two were on shaky ground anyway. Because her blaming herself for what she'd done per his request and him blaming himself for painting a target on Mason's cake? Not the best recipe for a healthy continuing relationship. I sadly hoped I was off the mark but I doubted it.

Carol just stared at me.

"Tell me about Ethan Perry." I needed to distract her and ask questions and this seemed like ideal timing. If anything was ideal at the moment.

She gulped and rubbed at the tears on her cheeks. I let go of my supportive grip on her arm and waited for her to pull herself together.

"He's a decent enough server," she said. "I'm aware, though, he's unhappy to be behind the scenes. Something about Mason not following through on his promise for a job teaching skiing or snowboarding or something."

So that was common knowledge. "Did he ever complain to you about Mason? Or do so in your hearing?"

"If he had," she said, "I'd have let him go immediately. No negativity about guests or owners, not in my kitchen. You're either happy to be here or you're out."

I liked her management style already. "Carol, this is important and I hope you remember."

Her grim expression had returned, eyes tight and no longer leaking tears. If anything, she'd reached for anger to help her regain control, though I wasn't sure that was the best choice for her. Not my call. "I already know what you're going to ask me," she said, "and yes. It was Ethan who took possession of Mason's dessert. Lucas insisted on it."

"Why?" *Was* Lucas part of this? If he made sure Ethan delivered it and Ethan was the killer...

"Because they were friends," she said, shrugging. "Lucas almost delivered it himself but I put an end to that. There was no need for him to grovel for that boy."

And now I knew what she really thought of Mason. Did that put her back on my suspect list? She could have been in collusion with Ethan, given him the oil. Still possible, yes, though I didn't buy her involvement. From the sound of things she wasn't willing to do anything to risk her relationship with Lucas and killing his son was a huge risk to take.

"Thank you for talking to me," I said. "I know the sheriff will have more questions when he gets to you." I wrinkled my nose at her as fair warning of Crew's pending interrogation. Though if he kept his typical rate of questioning—I'd been in his office almost two hours before Dad rescued me and Crew wasn't near done—the storm would be over, the plows through and spring arrived before he got to Carol.

She hugged me quickly as if she weren't sure her embrace would be welcome. I returned her squeeze with one of my own, heart in my throat.

"I'll be here," she said.

"One last thing," I said, turning to go. "Any idea where I might find Ethan now?"

She nodded crisply, clearly back under full Chef persona, at least for the moment. "I sent all of my staff to their quarters to wait for the sheriff," she said. "He'll likely be there."

Good to know. I exited the kitchen and headed down the hall to the foyer, pausing as I realized I had no idea how to access the staff quarters. Yes, I could have gone back and asked Carol, but when I spotted the front desk clerk crossing the foyer toward me, I nabbed her instead. At least this way I didn't have to feel like an idiot for forgetting.

"Miss Fleming," she smiled at me, her dark brown eyes glancing at the kitchen door and back to me while she paused at my request.

Wow, she remembered me. Great service. "I didn't get your name," I said, smiling back.

"Paisley Delaine," she said, shaking my hand with her own slim one, grasp firm but not too firm. Practiced and professional. I had a moment's thought she'd be perfect if I could poach her for the front desk of Petunia's before I shook off my traitor thought about the likelihood Daisy was leaving me and pressed on.

"I'm looking for the staff quarters," I said. "And Ethan Perry."

"Of course," she said, gesturing down the hall on the other side of the kitchen door. "If you go to the end of the corridor there's a white door on the left. You'll need a pass code to enter, though." She rattled off numbers so fast I laughed and shook my head. Paisley grinned with good nature, her long, blonde ponytail falling over one shoulder while she looked down and retrieved a pen from the inside pocket of her dark blue uniform jacket. I jotted the combination on the palm of my hand before handing the pen back to her.

"Thank you," I said. Paused. "Might be a random question, but the staff of places like this tend to get to know each other really well." She didn't respond to that so I pressed on. "Do *you* have any idea who might have wanted to kill Mason Patterson?"

She shook her head, looking sad suddenly. "I just started here last week," she said, tossing her hands a little, the palms softly slapping the cotton of her skirted thighs. "I've been working to learn all the systems and haven't had much chance to get to know anyone yet. Though, Mr. Patterson's presence was," she glanced around before finishing in a more hushed tone, "hard to miss."

"It was that." Not a good thing. And how quaint of her to be so reluctant to talk about him. Loyal too, huh? Hmmm.

Paisley nodded to me and started walking away before stopping with a soft sound of annoyance. "I'm so sorry," she said, turning to me once more, shaking her head. "I've been wrapped up in my work, my attention span is horrendous." She pointed out into the foyer. "I think I saw Noah and Ethan going into the bar, but I'm not sure. You might check there first."

That would save me a wasted trip to the staff quarters. "Thank you."

"Anything I can do to help," she said before hurrying off.

CHAPTER FOURTEEN

THE BAR FELT QUIET, bartender missing and likely sent to his own room to await Crew's endless interviewing. I didn't think I'd miss the soft strains of repurposed pop music that had filled the air, battling the sloshing waterfall of the feature that still spilled its endless wash down the far wall. I could only guess the stereo shut off when the power went out and needed to be reactivated, while the feature was on its own circuit. How special for it.

I quickly spotted the Perry brothers at the back of the room, huddled together talking at a table, a bottle of something they must have pinched from behind the bar between them. But only Noah had a glass, partially full, Ethan sitting back with his arms crossed over his chest and a furious look on his face.

Before I could interrupt, Ethan stood and stormed away from his brother, stomping past me. I left Noah staring after him and hurried to follow. That boy could hustle, my heels preventing me from running, so by the time I reached the foyer again he was disappearing around the corner toward the bathrooms. With a frustrated sigh I pursued him, almost tripping over the eager pug who came galloping toward me, promptly sitting on my feet the moment she reached me.

Not like Mom to lose sight of Petunia, but when my mother didn't show up, the big doors to the dining room firmly closed, I shrugged.

"She's not going to like the fact you escaped," I said. "In fact, she'll probably blame me."

Petunia grunted at me before farting and grinning her pug grin up at me, tongue hanging out.

"Fine, you can use that sniffer to chase down Ethan for me," I said, sliding my toes out from under her butt and heading for the side corridor. Petunia followed, waddling her way along and forcing me to slow down. I almost kept going, assuming Ethan had headed toward the staff quarters, only to hear the sound of a stall door slamming in the men's room.

Had to be him. And while I wasn't above just marching in and demanding answers, I did hesitate a moment. If he killed Mason, was it the best idea to just go in there and start ordering him to tell me what happened?

Petunia didn't give me the chance to think much past that initial nervousness. As the door opened—swinging inward at Ethan's angry hand—she darted between his legs and into the bathroom to his startled surprise. Knowing she'd just given me the perfect chance to question him, I laughed in embarrassment and forced him back into the bathroom with my body, wondering at my acting skills as I wrangled him almost expertly inside.

"I'm so sorry, she's such a brat." I slipped around him, the bathroom door closing behind him. "Would you please help me find her?"

He sighed quietly but nodded, peeking in stalls while I did the same.

"You're Ethan, right?" I beamed a smile at him. "Noah's brother?"

He grunted something, pausing and staring. "You're with the sheriff." That seemed to make him think twice, though he didn't turn threatening or try to leave. Instead, he just stood there, staring at me.

"I am." I dropped the pretense instantly. No need to insult his intelligence. "I just have a few questions, Ethan."

He shrugged, face twisting into anxiety and sorrow before settling into grim anger. "I didn't kill Mason. As much as I would have liked to on occasion."

"Like when he tried to poach your girlfriend," I said, "and gave your dream job to your brother?"

Ethan didn't say anything. He didn't need to.

"Why was Mason so into Ava, Ethan?" Someone smacked their lips. It was the weirdest sound to hear in a bathroom. The last stall was closed, door apparently locked. So we weren't alone in here. Whatever. I needed to keep pushing while Ethan felt vulnerable.

"Who knows," he said, hands clenching at his sides. "He never paid a bit of attention to her until..."

"Until she saved his life?" What would that mean to someone like Mason Patterson? That kind of selfless act might actually have penetrated the arrogant asshat he'd grown into.

Ethan's misery emerged on his handsome face. "He wouldn't leave her alone after that," he said, voice shaking. "She kept turning him down but I knew it was only a matter of time before his money and his offers for better jobs and opportunities would win."

"Like this job?" I waited for him to talk while the annoying smacking sound was punctuated with a fart. Ew, someone was having some serious gastric issues.

"He did this on purpose." He looked down at his uniform, back up to me. "I knew better than to let him get to me." Ethan's anger was back. "Yes, I would have preferred the ski job he offered me originally. But it was just a job, that's it. And Ava said she wanted nothing to do with him. I had no reason to kill him."

"Still, it must have burned, having to deliver his birthday cake to him." I liked Ethan for the murder, I couldn't deny it. Despite his heartbreak or maybe because of it. He really seemed the perfect candidate.

"I guess," Ethan said. "I had planned to dump it on his damned head. Screw this whole place and his bullying." He seemed to deflate then, turning to lean his back against the stall behind him, hands jamming into his pockets as he stared at himself in the mirror.

Dark bags like that on so young a face meant a long, terrible bout with self-doubt and sleeplessness. "I wanted to leave. Ava and I had plans to take positions in Aspen, even had jobs lined up. But Mason just kept pushing. She said it was only until the spring."

"And then?" What was wrong with the person in the last stall? Seriously, were they eating while they used the bathroom? That was just gross.

"New Zealand." I finally saw a flicker of joy in him. "For the summer. We both had dreams of following the snow, you know? Now, well." That excited anticipation died in a flare of sorrow and bitterness. "Now I have no idea."

"With Mason out of the way, there's nothing to stop you." That was heavy handed but I needed to prod him further.

He looked up at me, eyes so sad I flinched. "With Mason gone," he said, "and your sheriff looking at me for murder, there might be no Ava. And with no Ava, there's nothing."

Wow. Dedication worth killing for? I drew a breath to try to redirect the conversation and felt my heart thud once, painfully, as someone groaned in delight and farted again.

I spun, all attention on the last stall and the locked door, leaping for it and banging on it as I realized how stupid I'd been all this time. I'd lost track of the other occupant of this bathroom in my need to question Ethan, completely and utterly letting her fall out of my sight and my focus. And find something she most likely wasn't supposed to have.

"Petunia!" The locked door resisted my attempt to reach her. "What are you eating?"

Because it was her, it had to be.

Ethan lurched to my side, fingers working at the round, silver disk in the center of the door, jiggling it around until the latch released and the door swung violently inward. I stared in horror at the sight of my pug sitting sideways with her shoulder against the wall tile, licking at her chops and the oil dripping from her lips.

Next to her, lying on its side, was a tall, skinny brown bottle, crumpled plastic bag discarded beside it, a puddle of pale amber liquid spreading out beside the base of the toilet. A puddle she'd been happily consuming.

The men's room door opened and I turned to find Dad and Noah staring at me in surprise. Dad must have realized the look on my face meant trouble and hurried to us, squeaking to a hurried halt at my side before staring with wide eyed shock at the pug and her prize.

"I think," Dad said, trying not to smirk because it wasn't funny, damn it, "Madam Petunia has found our murder weapon."

She grinned up at him with her long tongue emerging, a mighty belch preceding a long and glorious fart.

CHAPTER FIFTEEN

"**T**HIS IS THE BOTTLE of oil from my kitchen." Carol examined the now plastic sealed container before handing it to Crew. "I have no idea how it ended up in the men's bathroom."

I had my suspicions. Considering I'd witnessed Ethan in this very washroom earlier with the out of order sign in place. An excellent opportunity to pour out a small sample to be tucked into his pocket and used on Mason's birthday cake before delivering it and tossing the evidence under Simone's chair to shift blame to my friend's sister.

Yeah, suspicions.

Crew tucked the plastic wrapped bottle into his tuxedo jacket pocket where it bulged awkwardly. "Mr. Perry, when I get this bottle fingerprinted, will I find yours on it?"

Ethan had been reluctant to join the conversation, though Dad hadn't given him a chance to argue. Now at least no longer in the men's bathroom, I leaned against the bar while the young waiter responded. Time to shed these shoes, taped toes or not. My feet hurt, my head hurt and I was pretty sure I knew who committed the crime.

"I've never seen that before," Ethan said, voice shaking. From guilt or just stress? "Besides, Mason's allergic. I avoided peanuts because of that. We all did."

"All of his friends," Crew said, sounding grave and understanding. "You're one of them, then? You're sure about that?"

Ethan fell silent, face tightening. "I know where this is heading," he said. "I want a lawyer."

"I'd love to grant you that request," Crew said, "but there aren't any here at the moment. So I guess that means you'll be spending the rest of this snowstorm confined to your room." He turned before I could protest, Dad scowling at the young waiter. "John, could you escort Mr. Perry to his quarters and make sure he can't leave?"

Dad grunted, looked unhappy. Because he thought Crew should push the kid despite lawyering up or because my father was, in effect, expected to take orders from the young sheriff? Whatever his protest, my father did as he was asked, gesturing for Ethan to precede him out the door.

"Crew," I slipped in beside him as my father and the young man left, Carol lingering, "I saw Ethan in the bathroom earlier, before dinner. There was an out of order sign on the door. Someone removed it after Ethan left, a maintenance man of some kind."

Crew's jaw jumped. "You were going to tell me this when?"

He did *not* just turn this on me. "Probably about the time I put two and two together and you had a minute to listen. That would be right now, in case you missed it."

He glared a moment before sighing and nodding, the tension leaving him while he rubbed at the throbbing vein on his forehead. At least his left eye twitch hadn't started yet. "Right," he said, tone softer. "Sorry, Fee. I'm just trying to wrangle everything and I forget sometimes you're not trained as an officer."

That was a sideways apology he'd pay for later. "Carol," I ignored him then, pissed he still tried to turn this back on me and knowing if I wanted to get anything done my continuing options were to do them my damned self. "What's the maintenance man's name? Tall, brooding, dark hair?"

"That's Bill," she said, grimaced. "Sorry, I don't remember his last name."

"Does he have a room in the staff quarters?" Maybe I could track him down and ask him about the sign. If he didn't place it there, it could be an indicator of Ethan's guilt.

"No," she said, frowning as she thought about it. "I think he has his own rooms by the ski lift near the maintenance shed, but don't quote me."

I was about to turn heel and leave when Crew nabbed my arm. "Where do you think you're going?"

It would have been so easy to snarl and spit and lose my temper. But I was brought up better than that. Instead, I twisted in his grip, using the self-defense methods my dad taught me, freeing myself quickly and facing him down. He really needed to learn that manhandling me wasn't an option ever. A lesson for another time.

"To find the answers you need," I said. "Unless you'd like me to go back to my room and leave you to handle this alone. Because I'm sure my dad would be more than happy to dump you on your ass, too, considering how you're treating a fellow officer like he's your lackey instead of your predecessor."

There it was, the eye twitch. My work here was done.

He didn't get to respond, though, not when three people burst into the bar.

"Why is my brother under arrest?" Noah might not have been full out drunk but he was well on his way, wavering a bit, forcing Ava and Simone to catch him before he stumbled forward into Crew. Nice distraction, I'd take it. Because my redhead temper had its limits.

"He's requested a lawyer," Crew said, all reasonable and crap, "which means I can't ask him more questions. But I have reason to believe he might be involved in Mason's murder, which forces me to confine him for the time being." Wow, was that so hard? Actually explaining? Clearly he had no problem doing so with others. Me, on the other hand? I had to piss him off to get him to give up anything.

"Ethan didn't kill Mason," Noah said while Ava's face crumpled.

"It's okay, Noah." She shot Crew a furious look. "We'll get him a good lawyer when the storm clears. It'll be all right. They have no proof."

"None of you are off the hook just yet," Crew said, voice dropping to the growling commanding sheriff tone that I think was meant to intimidate. Worked on the kids while I fought a snort of are you kidding me?

"By all means," Simone said, chin rising, "confine us to our rooms, too, if it makes you feel better. Ask us the same questions over and over again, because you'll get the same answers, I assure you." She'd noticed his badgering interrogation technique, apparently. Smart girl. "But while you do you let the real murderer wander free."

Crew drew a deep breath, visibly forcing his temper down. It was quite something to watch and I actually admired him for not cracking from the strain that crossed his face. When he spoke again, he was back to Captain Reasonable.

"You were all at the party where Mason almost died last time, correct?" They nodded together. "Including Ethan." More nods.

"What does that have to do with tonight?" Simone faltered, as if realizing she sounded ridiculous. The similarities of the situation were impossible to ignore. Birthday cake, peanuts and an injector pen. Only tonight ended a lot differently.

Crew was kind, though, and didn't go after her with disdain or sarcasm. Instead, he shrugged, body relaxing into a more confident and controlled stance. "Can you think of anyone else who might have a grudge against Mason, someone who knew of his allergy and is here tonight?"

They stared at him, mute in understanding. Because they had nothing.

"Ava," I said, interrupting exactly when I knew Crew would be pissed but having to ask. "Ethan said you two were going to Aspen, then New Zealand? Something about ski jobs?"

Noah snorted his tipsy denial while the young woman looked uncomfortable.

"As if," he said, arm around Ava's shoulders though without a trace of intimacy, more brother to sister or friend to friend as he squeezed her until she winced. "Right?"

"That was Ethan's plan," she said so carefully I felt terrible for the young man now confined and likely guilty of murder for this exact reason.

"But." Crew cut in, throwing me a shut it right now or you're out glare.

"Mason made me a great offer," Ava blurted, cheeks flushing. In embarrassment? Simone spun on her, fury clear, but Ava shook her head. "It's not what you think, Simmy."

Instead of waiting to hear her explanation, Simone stormed from the bar, clearly enraged. I needed to go after her. Even as Noah snorted one last time, leaning into Ava and booping her on the nose.

"Mason won, dude. As always."

Ava shoved him off and left herself, though whether to pursue Simone or Ethan I had no idea. But I took the distraction of Noah's sudden freedom and Crew's lunge forward to save him to escape the bar, grinning suddenly at the sound of the young man's stomach emptying in violent and noisy fashion.

I hoped he had excellent aim. Crew's shoes were just too shiny for their own good.

CHAPTER SIXTEEN

FUNNY HOW A CHANCE encounter can distract you from what you're supposed to be focused on. As I exited the bar I almost ran into someone entering, surprised to find Tom Brackshaw wandering around on his own. From what I knew the bank manager at Reading Savings Bank had no real ties to the lodge, though I could have been wrong. The likelihood he was a suspect in Mason's murder, however, seemed slim and when I paused and offered the obligatory smile, he smiled back, quickly seizing and shaking my hand with his own pudgy one as if actually delighted to see me.

I'd always liked Tom, found him friendly and kind, remembered being offered a sucker when I was a little girl and my parents brought me to his branch to open my first bank account. He had the same roundish face, if a bit rounder, the same circular glasses and less hair, but I'd know him anywhere.

"Fiona Fleming." His voice hadn't changed either, a warm tenor that rang with sincerity. He really was rather jolly for a banker. "How lovely to finally see you."

"Tom." I freed my hand. "Did you need something?"

He wrinkled his button nose at me, glancing in the bar and spotting Crew. "Ah, well. My mini-fridge is empty and I was hoping for a bit of something to tide me over while the storm rages." Tom winked a pale blue eye at me. He'd changed out of his own tuxedo and I wished I had thought to don my jeans and t-shirt. How casual he seemed, out of place without a suit on. "But I see the bar is occupied."

"Crew should be done shortly," I said. "As long as you return to your room after you find what you're looking for I'm sure he'll let it go." While the new sheriff likely would have wished he could just lock everyone in, without the manpower to police it the guests of the lodge were pretty much free to come and go as they pleased. He couldn't legally hold anyone he didn't charge and would be setting himself and the town up for a massive unlawful confinement class action if he tried. Though, it appeared everyone seemed reasonably willing to cooperate, I doubted he'd want their freedom of movement to be common knowledge. As for defending the contents of the bar, as far as I was concerned it was fair game. I wasn't in the mood to protect the lodge's alcohol at this point.

"Marvelous." Tom beamed at me before his eyes widened slightly, a quick drawn breath drawing me back before I could hurry away. "I've been waiting for you to come see me, young lady." He hesitated, face paling a little before he blurted his question. "I shouldn't speak out of turn. It's utterly against ethics and confidentiality, but your grandmother was an old friend and I know she was anxious to have the matter resolved once she'd passed. At least, according to her correspondence." He drew one last sharp inhale before leaning close with his bright eyes fixed on me like a little kid sharing a huge secret. "Fiona, did you ever find the key?"

And then my entire world crashed and went away and all I could do was gape at him. The key. From the metal box I dug up from the garden—that

Petunia dug up for me—that I'd guessed opened a safety deposit box. B-562. I'd found it months ago, the end of July, when Pete Wilkins died. Had intended all along to do something about it, got busy, fell into routine. But the *key*.

Tom chuckled at what had to be a dumbfounded look on my face. "Excellent," he said. "Your grandmother left me a letter over a year ago, telling me you'd be along for the contents of the box at some point. I wasn't sure if it was a mistake or not because you didn't show. But now I see you've simply forgotten."

I nodded, unable to speak. The mystery of the key at the bottom of the metal box with the love letters from Daniel Munroe, the dead husband of murderer Peggy Munroe. How? How had I let it go? "Do you know what's in it?"

He shook his head, cherub grin infectious. "No idea, my dear," he said. "And I couldn't reveal it to you even if I did. But I think it's time you found out."

I stood there as he eased past me and into the bar, now empty. Crew must have led Noah out the other exit. Not that it mattered right now as I tried to slow my heartbeat and remove the smile that pulled at my lips.

How could I have forgotten the mystery Grandmother Iris left for me? Life, I suppose. Excuses and time and work. Still. The second I had a chance, I'd be in Tom's office and I would uncover the truth of the key at last.

I have no idea why it felt so good to have that to hang onto as I turned toward the foyer and the entrance to the staff quarters. Except, maybe, it was my very own secret mystery with my grandmother, a gift from beyond the grave, and sometimes it was fun not to share.

All of that went away at the sound of shouting. Despite my heels I spun and ran, awkwardly to be sure, back into the foyer to find Ethan and Noah Perry screaming at each other while they did their best to land punches.

Ava hovered, Simone beside her, the two not helping any while they shouted for the brothers to stop. How Ethan had escaped Dad and Noah slipped away from Crew I had zero clue, but the two law men appeared from the dining room and, from their grim expressions, they wanted answers, too.

Between them they were able to pull the brothers apart, Noah's nose bleeding, Ethan panting with a cut over one eyebrow.

"I told you two to stay put," Crew said, face red. Embarrassed they hadn't listened? One was drunk, the other his main murder suspect and he thought a firm order would keep them confined.

"Don't look at me," Ethan scowled. "Noah broke the lock on our room and let me out."

"Just get over her already," Noah snapped as if he wasn't part of the same conversation at all, hoarse from puking, I could only imagine.

Ava's face darkened and she opened her mouth to speak but Ethan beat her to it.

"You don't know anything," he said, spittle flying as the intensity of his emotions got the best of him. Crew held him back with his arms through Ethan's, but the young waiter didn't fight him further, sagging in his grip while Noah shook free of Dad, wiping at his dripping nose.

"I know that you killed Mason to make sure Ava left with you," Noah said.

"And I think you killed Mason because he wouldn't forgive all the money you owed him."

Ethan stepped free of Crew after the sheriff slowly let him go.

Noah's face twisted in rage, gaze flickering to Crew and back. "You traitor."

"I owe you nothing," Ethan snarled. "You're not my brother. Not since you started hanging out with that piece of trash who bought your soul."

"You have no idea." Noah swayed, cracks showing in his drunken rage. "Mason was my best friend."

"You were freeloading off him and he'd had enough." Ethan chopped the air with one hand, blood flying from his knuckles. "And everyone knew it."

Ava stepped forward, hand on Ethan's arm but he shrugged her off.

"Please, Ethan," she whispered.

"Forget it." He backed away from her, hands in the air in surrender, face sad but still angry. "Don't you see, Sheriff? Lots of people had lots of reasons to hate that jerk and want him dead. People who pretended he was their friend." He seemed to absorb what he'd just said, his own words reaching him. "I should have walked away ages ago, Ava. But I trusted you. I was an idiot to believe you still wanted to be with me. I knew better. Everyone did. Thanks for making me the laughing stock of our friends all this time."

"I wasn't staying at the lodge job for Mason," she said, but Ethan wasn't hearing her. Neither, from the devastated look on Simone's face, was she.

Dad led Ethan away, Noah tipping his head back to stop the nosebleed and succeeding in losing his balance. I got to him first, steadied him, hoping his stomach was empty now and that more puking wasn't in his future. But he seemed much more stable than he had just a short time ago and I shook my head at the resiliency of youth. Yeah, because I was an old lady or something.

"Noah," I said, meeting Crew's eyes, "you were sitting right next to Mason, weren't you?"

Crew sighed like I'd just made his life more difficult, but it would have been impossible for him to miss the information Ethan gave up about Noah's relationship with the victim, so I was just handing the sheriff more ammunition, right?

"Let's go, Noah," Crew said, hand on the young man's arm. "You seem much more capable of talking than I first thought. Your turn to answer some questions." The sheriff glared at me as they headed for the dining room but I just crossed my arms over my chest, tilted my head at him and made sure he saw without a scrap of hesitation the amount of crap I gave he didn't like my interference.

Oh, snap.

CHAPTER SEVENTEEN

I TURNED SLOWLY AFTER Crew disappeared, attitude leaving me, thinking hard. There was more to the friend's circle than they were telling, I was sure of it. I really needed the means to investigate them without having to talk to them. And that meant snooping in their online lives. But in the middle of a snowstorm that knocked out the power?

Electricity meant possible internet connection. I spun and marched to the desk, smiling at Paisley who waved a little in her perky and friendly way as I leaned over the counter with a conspiratorial wink.

"Any chance there's Wi-Fi?"

She shook her head with a sad smile. "I'm sorry, we have nothing." She gestured at the TV behind her, blank and black. "Even the satellite is out, though I think it's likely just snow on the receiver. Bill is looking into it."

"The maintenance guy?" I bit my lower lip, thinking. "Do you know him very well?"

She frowned a little, then shook her head. "Not really," she said. "Aside from his name, Bill Saunders. I'm sorry, I'm not much help. He keeps to himself mostly, and we don't often see him in the lodge itself." She hesitated then, lips clamping together. "I don't usually make it a habit to talk about people I work with."

I nodded, seeing her reticence and knowing she had something juicy. "Spill it. I won't tell."

She seemed to relax at that. "I hate gossip, but Bill's not a bonded employee." Bonded. What, he had a record? Interesting.

"Thanks for that," I said. "Anything else you think of, let me know, okay?" If Bill was an ex-con, could he have reason we didn't know about to target Mason? And why would this place even consider hiring a non-bondable employee when surely there were tons of people who could take the position? Lots of questions to chase down.

"Thanks for the help," I said, knowing I had one option for an online search left. "You're doing a great job." I don't know why I said that, except that she'd been keeping her cool and working hard, at least from what I could see, since I got here and that was the sign of a great work ethic. I fully intended to approach her about shifts at Petunia's when this was over.

She flushed, looked down, but she was smiling. "Thank you," she said so softly I almost didn't hear her. "That means a lot."

I left her with the compliment still making her grin and headed for the stairs. Yes, I could have used the elevator to go to my seventh floor room, but my luck? The stupid genset would die and I'd be trapped in there for the rest of the investigation. Storm. Same thing.

Instead, I slipped off the horribly uncomfortable heels and, with a satisfying tug at the tape to free my toes and now in my bare feet, climbed the endless walk to my floor. The stairwell felt quiet, too quiet, echoing as I accidentally tapped the heels against the metal railing. Whoever designed the stairwell didn't expect anyone to have to use it, obviously, because the concrete and steel wasn't in keeping with the ultra lush and luxurious design of the rest of the lodge.

Cutting corners, were they? Well, Pete Wilkins had been part of the construction, so they were lucky the place didn't fall apart. Come to think of it, maybe that was inevitable as it had finally been proven after all Dad's hard work Pete's company was shirking on materials and skimming the extra funds.

I made it upstairs and into the main floor hall, found my room down the endless corridor, the keycard I tucked into my bra working on the third try. Again, good thing the generators were functioning because there'd be a lot of trapped guests if something happened to them. I needed to mention that to Dad. And had a moment of sympathy for Olivia in all this.

The mayor had to be having a hissy fit by now.

My phone lay on the bed, still messy from Daisy's attempt to make me gorgeous—a success, thanks—the corner just visible under the edge of the t-shirt I'd discarded. I sank into the soft mattress, crossing my bare legs and turning the phone on, checking my data. And finding bars. Would wonders never cease. I actually squeaked out a little war cry of delight and fist pumped the air before hopping onto social media and searching for Mason Patterson.

He was easy enough to find, the selfie king of every freaking app I looked at. I wasn't judging or anything, but can you spell narcissist?

But what I was seeing really didn't tell me more than I already knew. I needed inside his accounts. And I knew someone who might have access. After second guessing the chance to change I made a compromise in favor of haste and slid my feet into a pair of flats I'd brought only to be poo-pooed by Daisy. Well, my toes were happier and so was I as I hurried out of my room and to the stairwell, heading back down to the foyer. And paused at the top of the stairs on seven. I had no idea where Simone's room was, where she was now. But there was a quick way to find out.

Holla, Jazz, I texted quickly in the quiet of the stairwell, the soft beeping as I tapped echoing in the silence. *You have Simone's number handy?*

The instant I sent it off I second guessed my choice. She'd know something was up. I was terrible at hiding anything from her. If she tried to call instead of texting I was dead in the water. Idiot, I could have just gone back downstairs and looked for Simone instead of bothering my friend.

Too late. It was literally three seconds between me hitting send and my friend's response and I was a goner.

FEEFEE. Sigh. I hated nicknames, but how could I reject that one when it came from tall, happy and awesome? At least she didn't call me Fanny. *Hugs, woman. Simmy squeeze you yet?*

Phew. So she didn't know or suspect anything, wicked. I just had to keep it that way. The fact I didn't have six million texts waiting already told me Simone kept her mouth shut. Now it was my turn.

You bet, I sent. Awkward, two words like that. Seriously?

Good think awkward was my regular state. She tagged a phone number on the end of her next text and I quickly shot off a query to Simone while answering her sister. *Like, giant squeezes?*

Biggest squeezes outside yours, I sent. *Thanks, gotta run.*

That was short, Jazz sent back as I waited for her sister to respond. And, just when I thought I'd avoided disaster, I go and step in it. *Everything kosher?*

I could have told her then. Probably should have despite knowing it would end in screaming and phone calls and Simone hating me forever because I tattled. Not to mention worrying one of my dearest friends from a time when friends had been a scarce commodity thanks to Ryan. But since Simone hadn't said anything to Jasmine, it really wasn't my place. I had to smooth this over. Still, I ached with guilt as my fingers typed then hovered a moment over send before I winced and responded. Hoped I hit the right note of airy nothing with my next text.

All good, I sent, exhaling as I finished. *Partying in Reading, you know. Luvs.* Hit send. Waited, worried, pictured her freaking out and not believing me and not being able to do anything actually helpful while losing her massive mind.

Then, ding. *Have all the FUN. Wish I was there. MWAH.* And Jazz was gone.

CHAPTER EIGHTEEN

I DIDN'T HAVE TIME to linger over my betrayal, though, because my phone whistled once more and the number Jazz gave me appeared.

Bar, Simone sent. *Hiding.* ☹

I ran down the steps, out of breath but feeling rejuvenated from the rush of adrenaline as I pushed through the doors and into the lobby, heading directly for the bar and Simone. She was tucked into the back corner, head in her hands when I sank into the soft padding of the bench seat and hugged her.

Simone leaned into me, weeping softly, her hands clutching at me and I held her a long moment, chin on the top of her head, wishing there was something

I could say. But her boyfriend was dead, she was a suspect and, though I knew she didn't do it, I also understood from experience how devastating it was to be fingered for murder. And, from the sound of things, that same boyfriend wasn't faithful, though to be honest it seemed he'd never claimed to be anything but a player, at least in his public life.

Simone finally leaned away, using a cloth napkin to wipe her cheeks and the drips from her round chin. "Thanks for that," she choked, tried a smile. "I was going to stay in my room like the sheriff asked but I just couldn't. I had to get out of there. All the staff are talking, about Ethan and me and Ava." She blew her nose before tossing the used napkin back to the table. "This is the worst night of my life." Simone tried a brave smile. "It means a lot, knowing you're here."

"Anytime," I said. "Then again, do your best not to be accused of murder from now on, okay?"

She laughed, so I'd hit the right note after all. Simone squeezed my hand before cocking her head at me, her sleek, black hair shining in the light. "How did you get my number?"

"Jazz," I said and then held up my free hand to silence her fearful protest. "I lied to her and told her everything was okay. I swear." She nodded, looked down at the crumpled and makeup stained napkin. "You'll have to tell her eventually, obviously, but it can wait until the hotel isn't locked in a snowstorm. Because knowing Jazz she'd hitch up sled dogs and Nanook of the North her way here to kick ass and save her little sis. Before murdering the two of us."

That made both of us laugh. "I can totally see it," Simone said, big smile making me happy. And then she sighed and sagged back into the cushions. "What am I going to do, Fee? I didn't kill Mason."

I handed her my phone. "Do you have access to his social media accounts?"

She frowned at me but took possession, long nails tapping on the screen. "He didn't seem to care who had his passwords," she said, handing the phone back a moment later. "But what does his online stuff have to do with his death?"

"I don't know yet," I said, "but this might give me a clue to find out who really did kill him." I paused, winced. "Simone, do you think Ethan did it?"

Her face crumpled as she fought off tears. "I don't know," she said. "We all arrived in January, just after Christmas. The jobs Mason got us were sweet, you know? I was basically a glorified guide, got to wear the cutest uniform out on the hill, didn't really work much, just looked pretty for the guests." She shrugged, apology in her expression. "Like our jobs were made up out of the blue to give us all something to do."

"All but Ethan." Wow, what an ego blow.

"Well, and Ava. She took her teaching position seriously." Simone didn't seem impressed by that at all. "It was a cushy thing, just for a few months, a chance to take a break from school."

"Your parents must have been pissed." I'd met Jazz and Simone's folks, both hard working, both white collar and dedicated to their daughters. Loved their big voices and strong beliefs and stunning brownstone in New York.

"Jazz was the most against it," Simone said, sounding small and frail. "Mom actually told me to go. Get this out of my system so I could focus on school."

Good for her. "Did it work?"

She blew a long breath between her full lips. "Not in the way she expected, but yeah." Simone's big eyes met mine. "I can't wait to go back to college."

I bet. "Ethan, Simone."

My friend's sister swallowed hard, like she didn't want to answer. "I don't want to think he had anything to do with Mason's death," she said. "But I worry he might have. He was so angry, Fee. I adore Ethan, he's a great guy. And Ava is awesome. Noah's been a dick since Mason started calling him his bestie, but those two are my closest friends." She lost her sadness and anger flickered. "Were. Now that I know Ava was lying all along and planned to stay at the lodge. I guess you just never really know people."

I had my doubts about Ava's motivations, but didn't bother arguing with Simone. Instead, I tucked in closer to her and started looking through Mason's accounts. She took interest when I prodded her and answered questions when I asked.

"That's the common room in the house Mason rented for us at college," Simone said of the first photo I held up to her. "Party." She shrugged at the mass of people, Mason's grinning face and the usual suspects around him. "Nothing unusual."

Three more photos from the same event and I noticed a trend. "Who's that?" While the face was hard to make out, the blue hoodie with the school logo didn't change, nor the glasses and dark hair. Lingering in the background in every photo at the party. I switched to another night—clear from the alteration in wardrobe—and found the exact same lurker in the background, this time in a bulky red sweater.

Simone frowned over the images but shook her head at last. "There's tons of people who came to Mason's parties," she said. "He'd announce them on his social media and the house would fill up and that was it. No real planning or anything."

"And he almost died at one of those parties?" I kept scrolling.

"Last birthday," she said. "Before we left for Aspen." And she flinched.

"And Elizabeth Adler disappeared," I said. And pointed to the lurker. "Is that her?"

Simone squinted but sighed at last. "I honestly didn't know her very well. I wasn't in Mason's inner circle at that point." She sounded embarrassed by that. "Here." She took out her own phone from the small bag she carried, skimmed through her photos then handed the device to me. "That's Elizabeth."

She certainly looked like the lurker with dark hair and glasses. An unfortunate nose and acne that lingered despite her age. I hated to bring it up, but… well. "She doesn't seem Mason's friend type." And now I was going to hell for judging the poor girl because I was sure she was perfectly nice and all that and I was looking at her picture and making assumptions.

But Simone's sad face told me I was right. "She was... awkward. And kind of in love with Mason. Embarrassed herself a lot." Sigh. "She hung out with us because of him, because Lucas asked him to be nice to her for James's sake. But she was more a source of amusement for Mason than really liked, if you know what I mean." She met my eyes with her own full of guilt and I realized Simone did nothing to stop what had to have evolved into bullying for her to look so uncomfortable.

Someone cleared their throat, making us both jump. I looked up to find Paisley standing there, watching us. She waved off our startled reaction with a soft smile of apology before speaking.

"I'm so sorry to interrupt," she said, "but I think our internet is working now if you'd like to try the Wi-Fi."

"All good," I said, waving my phone at her. "But thank you so much." Poaching her for sure now.

Paisley paused before leaving, her sympathy clear as she nodded to Simone. "I'm sorry about your friend," she said. Simone didn't comment, just hung her head. I hated to think she was ignoring the young woman because she was the help, but that's what it felt like.

"You're very kind," I said, shattering the discomfort of the moment. "Thanks, Paisley."

She nodded to me then walked away with that efficient and professional gait of hers.

Now wasn't the time to kick Simone's ass for being rude, but I really, really wanted to. There'd be opportunity later—and a chat with Jasmine first. Because while I would do anything to protect the young woman sitting next to me, she did not get to be a bitch because she'd been hanging out with the wrong people.

Okay then. Onward.

CHAPTER NINETEEN

I LEFT SIMONE TO go in search of James and ask him if he recognized the girl in the photos. If it was Elizabeth that had been the lurker I was chasing down a ghost. But if someone else was in that photo, could they hold a grudge against Mason? Maybe a friend of Elizabeth's? It was a long shot and actually stirred something inside me. A thought that I tried to shake while it built and built in my mind and wouldn't let me go.

I was almost to the staff door when I paused and really thought about it. What if Elizabeth didn't die after all? No, that was dumb. But my feet wouldn't move and I lingered near the large double doors with the red glowing exit sign over them, staring up into the illuminated letters and not seeing them. If she survived, she would have told her father, come forward. Someone would have said something. But what if she couldn't? Forgot who she was? No, that didn't work either. Revenge was a powerful motivator, though, wasn't it? And maybe the chance of insurance money if James was in the kind of trouble he said he was, being pushed out of the lodge like he claimed. If Elizabeth did get in touch with her father and decided to kill Mason in revenge for leaving her on that mountain...

Well. Now I was attributing murder to ghosts.

Shaking my head, I turned toward the staff door and away from the big ones marked with the exit sign, just as something rustled, like leaves in a wind, and the lights died again. Crap, that was all I needed. I stumbled forward, the faint red glow of an emergency light flickering and dying over the staff door, leaving me in total darkness.

I had just turned to head back toward the foyer when something hit me hard in the shoulder, driving me sideways and into the double doors at my right. I cried out in surprise as the way parted, a chill wash of snow hitting me, wind buffeting against me while, shock taking over, I collapsed sideways into the snowbank on the other side when the door slammed shut behind me.

I lay in the snow a moment, surprise leaving me rigid, before stumbling to my feet, tucking into the narrow corridor between the bank and the door, the wind creating a tiny cleared space along the edge of the building. Already freezing and shivering, bare legs coated in snow, I pounded on the door, panic grasping me by the chest and squeezing.

There were no handles on this side. Just the sealed center of the pair of metal doors. And no bell or any other way to contact those inside and let them know I was out here. Which, I could only guess while I struggled to figure out what to do past my terror that grew by the instant, wind and snow howling around me, was the point.

My phone was gone, lost in the snowbank and I knew better than to waste time trying to find it. While I wasn't much of a skier, I had taken basic safety and understood I had about five minutes before frostbite started, give or take not knowing the temperature and not really caring, thanks. And maybe six to eight before my body started to lose feeling and begin procedure to protect my core from freezing. All that time to make my way around the building while shivering uncontrollably in slippery flats and a mini-dress and to a door that would open.

Easy. Okay. One step at a time. I would not give in to panic and the icy storm that made visibility impossible. My freezing fingers held contact with the wall beside me as I abandoned the doorway, chose a direction, and walked as fast as I could through the snow, using the wall to keep me from falling again. Because if I fell, I wasn't sure I'd be able to get up.

I reached a corner far faster than expected and realized my mistake as I tried to continue. While the wind made a nice channel for me to slip and slide along on the far side, that same wind instead tucked all the snow up against the wall of the lodge and instead of a way through I faced a huge wall of snow.

I've only faced utter despair a few times in my life and this, I'm not embarrassed to say, was one of them. The instant I accepted that I wasn't going anywhere and had to turn around felt like the biggest failure I'd ever faced. And, honestly, for a brief moment I almost gave in to the cold. Because I was going to die out here, freeze to death before I could make it back even to the door I'd been pushed out of. I had already lost feeling in my feet, my fingers, my nose, ears. And the pounding of my heart as it labored to keep me warm, the closing in of the blackness around my vision, all signs. How long had I been exposed? Was it five minutes already? My mind went into logic mode, whispering to me what to expect while my heart hoarded blood in an effort to keep me warm. Soon, I'd start to feel like the temperature had risen as my body shut down, that I was at a normal heat again instead of turning into a Feecicle. I'd fall into a snowbank and close my eyes and go to sleep forever and they might find me in the spring if a bear didn't drag me off and use me for a snack.

Silly. Bears hibernated for the winter. Maybe a fox or a coyote then. Wolf? Something hungry.

All of this flashed through my head as the howling wind tore at my updo and my ridiculous dress and up my skirt while desperately angry tears wet my eyes. Death stared me in the face, icy fingers pulling me into oblivion. And with a swear word I learned from my dad—and the kind of fortitude I knew he'd never let me live down if I failed—I turned my back on the storm and retraced my wobbling, weakening and slowing steps.

I didn't even flinch when my first thought of being a large animal meal came true and a giant black bear burst into sight and leaped for me. Maybe it would hurt when he ate me, and maybe not. I was so cold I actually couldn't find a give a crap. I tumbled sideways when he landed at my feet, into the snow at last, whispering an apology to my dad for not being strong enough in the end.

My feet hurt, my hands too, tingling with the kind of painful pins and needles that drove gasps from my lips and forced my eyes open. I stared into the quiet of the small room, the fire across from me crackling in happy snaps and pops, heavy weight of blankets wrapped around me so tight I felt suffocated. But warmth returned and with it the kind of shivering bout that made my teeth rattle in my mouth.

Alive. But how? A shaggy black head popped up next to me where I lay on what had to be a bed, giant pink tongue swiping my cheek, wet nose pressing into my neck.

"Moose, leave off now, boy." I didn't know that voice but at least understood the black bear who'd come to eat me wasn't a bear after all. The massive Newfoundland dog leaned away, kind, brown eyes never leaving me, velvet ears perked as someone sat next to me and offered a steaming mug with big, rough hands. "Drink."

I tried to sip, coughed when the hot coffee caught in my throat, but took another taste right away as the warmth of it shot down into my stomach and helped still some of the shivering. Within a minute I was sitting up, the blankets that smelled enough like dog I knew Moose had to sleep on them too wrapped around me and drank on my own, shaking hands both clasped around the hot mug and making them ache as blood flow returned.

"You're lucky Moosey found you," the big man said, stepping away to sink into a rocking chair next to the fire. Bill Saunders, the maintenance man with the record, if Paisley was right. Had to be. I recognized him from earlier tonight. Was it really just one night? I had no idea what time it was now, but it felt like the longest evening of my life. "You were near to frostbite and hypothermia out there. My place was the closest and I have a fire." Was that anxiety in his voice? "Hope it's okay I brought you here." Apparently that was a yes to his nervousness.

Regardless of his concern, gratitude was my only emotion at the moment. I nodded over my mug.

"Thank you for the rescue," I said. "I can assure you I wasn't out in the snow on purpose."

He didn't comment on that. "You're John Fleming's daughter." His voice was as deep and as rough as his hands, almost expressionless, as if he expected to be rejected or berated.

"I am," I said. "You know my dad?"

"Used to," he said. Paused. "He put me away."

Score one Paisley. An ex-con for real. Hard to judge the man who just saved my life, though. Or think he could be a murderer, not when I was finally getting warm and his sweet dog watched me with gentle eyes. "You been out long?" I tried to keep my voice level while Moose continued to stare at me, tongue out. He was huge, but kind and he clearly loved his master, so I chose to trust as the dog trusted.

"A year," Bill said, adding a log to the fire in the potbelly stove. Sparks leaped and flames flared a moment. "I know how this looks."

What did that mean? "You saving my life? Yeah, I'd say that looks pretty good from here."

He didn't accept the offer of humor, sighing instead. Moose left me at last, went to his master and shoved his big noggin under Bill's hand. The equally large man scratched his dog's ears until he groaned as he spoke again, voice dropping even deeper and full of hurt.

"I know what happens when everyone finds out there's a murder and an ex-con in the same place at the same time," he said. "And as soon as you're up to it, we'll go find your dad and I'll turn myself in."

CHAPTER TWENTY

WAIT, WHAT? "YOU KILLED Mason Patterson?" But, why? I almost dumped the last of the precious coffee, heart pounding, suddenly not so comfortable with the giant man/dog combination. My brain stuttered, needing clarification. I was alive. He could have left me out there to die. Not the act of a murderer, was it?

Bill shook his head, refused to look at me. "I didn't hurt Mason," he said. "He was my friend. But that young sheriff will think it was me because I used to be in prison. That's how these stories always end. So I'll just save everyone the trouble of saying the ex-con did it."

Chest aching with more than the cold that had almost killed me, I found my eyes stinging with new tears. "Tell me about how you ended up working here," I said.

Bill looked up at last, dull brown eyes meeting mine and for a moment I wondered if he was even going to answer. Then, he sighed again but only after Moose nudged him in the hand for stopping his endless petting. Bill resumed scratching the dog's ear and spoke.

"I had a job at the college for a bit," he said. "Then some professor accused me of stealing from his office. Well, it wasn't me." Bill sounded angry at last, offended. "They fired me lickety split even though they caught his cute little assistant with his stuff. Because can't have an ex-con hanging around even though I just wanted a job."

"So Mason offered you one here?" It had to be hard. Discrimination against former criminals wasn't a shock or anything. "Why?"

Bill shrugged, rubbing a finger over the bridge of his flat nose he'd broken a time or two in the past and healed crooked. "Dunno. Just kind of hit it off with him from the start. He'd crack jokes, buy me coffee. When he found out I was fired he offered me this job right away." Bill's face tightened. "I know a lot of folks didn't like Mason none, but he was good people down deep where it mattered."

If he said so. And honestly, the man clearly had a different experience with the kid, so fair enough. "And you've been here ever since?"

He shifted in his chair, seemed to relax a little, probably because I wasn't accusing him of murder. "He made a point to come check on me earlier tonight before dinner." His voice cracked, one hand wiping his eyes before he set his narrow lips in a thin line against his emotions, visible in the tension of his body. "Meant a lot."

Well, so maybe I could cut Mason a little slack if he showed such empathy to a man who received none from others. "Thank you for saving me," I said, as kindly and with as much genuine gratitude as I could. Because I really, really meant it.

"You're welcome." A faint smile? I'd take it. "How'd you end up outside in that getup?"

I shook my head, finishing my coffee and staring into the empty bottom of the mug. "Someone cut the lights in the back hallway and then pushed me outside and locked the doors behind me."

He grunted. "They auto lock."

"Who would know that?" I looked up and met his troubled frown.

"Staff," he shrugged. "That door leads to the back entry to the ski lifts. The instructors use it sometimes as a short cut even though I tell them not to."

"I'm lucky you were out there," I said. "And Moose."

He patted the big dog on the head who panted his happiness up at his master. "He's a good dog," Bill said. "I was making my rounds, almost didn't go out because of the storm."

I made a connection as he frowned. "The missing snowmobile," I said, remembering he mentioned it to the GM, Donna Walker, earlier. "You were looking for it out there? In this weather?" Wow, this place knew how to attract loyal staff. Maybe there was a spot for Bill at Petunia's too.

"I hate having things out of place," he grunted. "Last I looked it was there, then just gone like that." His big fingers snapped. "I didn't want Mason to think I'd stolen it or anything. Because I didn't."

"Bill." I drew a breath and swallowed before speaking again, needing to know before we headed back into the fray inside. "I need to ask you what you were in prison for." His face fell and I watched his small, infant trust for me vanish. But before he could shut down completely, I went on. "I know you didn't kill Mason and I'm going to tell Crew and Dad that. But if I'm aware of what crime you committed, it'll be easier to defend you."

Bill hesitated before nodding like he'd given up at last. "It's not good," he said.

That told me what I needed to know. "You were in for murder," I said.

The big man met my eyes with his own brown gaze flat. And that answered that question.

CHAPTER TWENTY-ONE

EXCEPT, APPARENTLY, IT DIDN'T. Because Bill finally leaned forward, hugging Moose's big, furry head to his chest and stared into the flames as he spoke in a voice suddenly shifted from deep and deadened to full of remorse.

"I had too much to drink that night," he said, "like every other night. But this night instead of just me in the car? Yeah, I had to have that one more beer before I went to the rink to pick up my boy."

I knew where this was going and almost stopped him but Bill rocked a bit and hugged his dog like he was his son while the fluffy Newfoundland whined and licked his master's face.

"I fell asleep, been working a twelve hour at the plant. Took the extra because of the money, right? And thought a few beers were a great way to wind up the day. Had to go back out to get the kid anyway. Buckled him in the back, only ten years old." He didn't look away from the fire. "At least I only killed him when I hit that pole on the other side of the ditch. Could've ruined another family's lives that night if I'd crossed the median. Instead, I walked away with a concussion and the shakes and my son died on impact when a tree branch came through his window and punctured his heart."

I wept for him because he wouldn't cry, that poor, broken man who sat in front of his fire with his big dog as his only comfort. Maybe Bill had already shed the tears he intended to or perhaps he'd never been able to find the strength to let himself be that vulnerable. So I snuffled and hiccupped and wiped at my own tears while he sat back again and waited for me to be done.

"Your dad was first on scene, treated me decent despite what I'd done. And the judge was kind," Bill said into the sound of the fire snapping. "Gave me manslaughter, but I knew it was murder. Premeditated, though I never wanted to kill my own boy." There was the hitch in his voice, the catch of hurt. "But still, I knew the risks every time I drank and drove. And I did it anyway." He looked at me at last. "Ten years with good behavior. And I behaved. Gave up drink, haven't touched a drop since. Got myself a mechanics diploma, worked hard to learn a trade. My wife's long gone, divorced me over Teddy and I hardly blame her that. Hear she remarried and moved to Texas." And just like that he'd laid out his whole life to me, a gift.

"No matter your past, Bill," I said, "you're no murderer. And if there's evidence you killed Mason, I've yet to see it."

He nodded to me. "Thanks for that," he said, grunting to his feet. He couldn't have been much over fifty but moved like a man carrying decades more than that. "We'd best get you inside and cleaned up."

I could only imagine how horrible I looked but couldn't care less. Sure, I could have stood on my own—told myself so anyway—but it was nice to grasp his big, rough hand, to be guided to my feet, shaking legs holding me upright. I took a minute to examine my extremities, knowing how lucky I was not to see deadened white tips on my toes and fingers. Okay, or deadened Fee in a snowbank outside the lodge. Whatever. Gratitude washed through me in a wave and I hugged Bill tight around the waist, the closest thing I could reach. I thought my dad was tall.

He tentatively embraced me back with a gentle pat to my shoulder before letting me go. The smile he shared then was sweet and kind and I beamed up at him before bending to hug Moose in turn.

"Good boy," I said, kissing his soft doggy nose.

"Mason," Bill said while I stood, wobbly and a bit dizzy still, catching me with both hands steadying me with the most respectful caution before letting me go again. "He died from his allergies?"

I nodded, accepting his arm as he turned toward the door. This had to be his apartment, his personal space. It didn't look anything like what I imagined, one corner filled with spare parts and mechanical implements he was clearly working on. "We believe someone laced his cake with peanut oil."

Bill grunted. "I get my meals in the kitchen, but Chef chases me when I'm done so I'm no help there. Didn't see anyone or anything." He sounded disappointed.

"Earlier tonight you took an out of order sign off the men's washroom outside the foyer," I said.

Bill nodded this time, eager as he opened the door and waited for me to exit. It was cold on the other side and he flinched before turning back, nabbing a big, heavy gray sweater off a hook before draping it around me. The scent of Moose and petroleum products embraced me along with the itch of wool but the warmth was welcome. Noise I hadn't noticed earlier rumbled close by, sounding like a fleet of airplanes approaching. "This part of the building's not insulated," he said. He turned and gestured and though Moose whined at us he settled on his fuzzy butt and stayed put when Bill closed the door. Pointed down the hall away from his door. "Generator room is that way." Was he enjoying the idea of showing someone his domain? We headed the opposite direction of the noise. Leaving the chill of the hall and its rough, unfinished design and passing into more carefully presented area painted and decorated to match the lodge colors, Bill pointed up at the ceiling. Giant chain and gears loomed overhead as we walked, entering a large space with signs and warnings about how to safely use the equipment. "We're under the ski lift." A large garage like door at the far end stood closed against the elements, silent chairs stacked in a line waiting to come to life and begin their endless round up and down the mountain.

Interesting at any other time, and I wasn't adverse to nodding and smiling most times. But he hadn't answered my question. "The out of order sign," I prompted gently.

"Right!" Bill moved fast and I hurried to keep up, shivering all over again but seeing the door we headed for. To the staff quarters had to be, another at the far end painted the same as the walls, maybe to outside? From the skim of snow at the bottom I was pretty sure that was the case. A corridor led off past it with an arrow and "Lodge Foyer" in pretty font pointing to the main part of the building.

Bill quickly tapped numbers on the keypad next to the door to the staff area and it opened, the same numbers Paisley had written on my hand earlier. "This way's warmer." I appreciated that immensely. "I didn't know why the sign was on the bathroom. I hadn't put it there. I took a quick peek but everything was okay, so I took it away. I didn't get a call or anything."

"Are you the only one who does that kind of thing?" Surely there was a big maintenance staff?

But Bill shrugged. "I manage," he said. "There's a couple of part timers who come in during the day, but I live on site so I take care of most things myself." That sounded like the beginning of pride.

"You're obviously very good at what you do," I said. Because a little self-esteem boost did a heart good.

Bill's smile told me I was right again. Yes, nice staff. Mine soon.

"Don't get me wrong, Miss Fleming," Bill said as he pulled the staff door shut behind him, the heat of the main building embracing me. I handed back his sweater, still feeling weak and tired but far better than the alternative. "Mason wasn't a good person most of the time. But it wasn't his fault. That mother of his was a bad seed, her whole side of the family. Mr. Lucas did his very best to make sure Mason felt like he was his real father. I saw it all the time, even if Mason didn't." So Lucas did care for the boy. I trusted Bill's judgment and outsider perspective on instinct. He reminded me too much of my dad not to. "I don't want to paint him as a saint, because he wasn't. But he had a good side not many got to see."

I wasn't really listening to Bill just then. Not out of rudeness or reluctance, but sheer distraction. Now that I was safe and inside the staff quarters, I could try to forget what just happened, stuff it down under making solving this murder my priority. But standing here in the safety of the lodge triggered the kind of fear I hadn't yet processed. Terror at my near death experience almost dropped me to my knees as I finally accepted how close I'd come to dying out there in the snow.

So I'd talk to Ava again, Simone, everyone who might have answers, sure would. Right after I dug around inside me and triggered enough anger I could function. While hunting down security footage and figuring out who tried to kill me.

CHAPTER TWENTY-TWO

ILL FELL SILENT THEN, didn't say a word as we travelled the short hallway past a large pair of doors to what had to be communal bathrooms and out into the main corridor again. Had my own silence cut off his willingness to speak? I didn't know but hadn't the strength to put him first when my stomach churned about as fast as my mind.

Helped to look around and force myself to be curious, even a little. This whole area, while tidy and finished, didn't have the kind of polished perfection of the main lodge. Plain gray carpet and ordinary white walls with a few signs dotting the emptiness with directions to bathrooms and the main lobby were punctuated by someone's vain attempt at décor with a few stock photo posters in cheap frames. Clearly the builders hadn't thought esthetic appeal important when it came to staff. The corridor we walked turned to the right, set with multiple plain white doors with placards beside them bearing names in magic marker.

I hoped the staff quarters themselves were a bit less stark.

We finally emerged into the main corridor of the lodge, the difference in appearance instant as the thicker carpet gave under my feet, the towering ceilings and ice palace feel a bit overwhelming after what I'd just endured. I kept Bill between me and the large double doors I'd been pushed through, hurrying despite my weakness as fast as I could toward the foyer. Bill paused before I was comfortable, next to one of the large plants that bracketed the men's washroom and pulled the leaves aside. The rustling sound I'd heard before the lights went out, a coincidence? Only then did I realize the shrubbery was fake. Ah, deception and disappointment, how wretched. But my cynicism faded to surprise as he revealed a gray panel hidden behind the plastic foliage. So that sound had been a warning, if I'd known what I was hearing.

"Whoever cut the power used this for cover," he said, and I nodded as I imagined it would be easy enough. I'd been distracted, in a hurry and the fake plant was thicker than a real one would have been, tall enough to conceal even Bill's substantial height. "This panel controls the power in this end of the lodge." He flipped the door open, squinted inside. "Everything looks fine." Crew's people could fingerprint it later. "If they knew what they were doing it wouldn't take much to cut the power to everything, including the emergency beacon and exit sign."

Tidy explanations gave me a bit of relief from what I'd just endured, helped settle my mind. Not that it could stop the meep of utter relief at the sight of my mother—Petunia trotting at her feet—and Dad heading toward me when I turned away from Bill who snapped the panel shut again.

I lurched out of his shadow and hugged Mom tight, feeling her embrace as desperate as my own.

"Fiona," she gasped into the mess that was my hair, "what happened to you?"

I caught Dad's terrified and then furious expression as he turned on Bill.

"Bill Saunders," Dad said with that judging tone he used when he thought he was right about everything. "I didn't know you'd moved back to town after you were released." Oh, he was thinking bad things about my rescuer, I could see it in his face. While Bill shrank back, head down, ready to cut and run and I didn't blame him a bit.

I jerked free of Mom long enough to smack Dad in the shoulder before bending to scoop Petunia for a hug and a few licks while my heart tried to settle and tears fought my need to keep it together. "Bill saved my *life*," I choked. So much for not crying.

Dad gaped at me, Mom shaking while I told them everything between initial sobs before I managed to seize my surging emotions in a vice-like grip, grasping the maintenance man's green work sleeve and holding onto him to keep him with me so he'd hear everything. I wanted him to know I trusted him and when I finished, Dad stuck out his hand and firmly shook Bill's in his own with the kind of vigor that he reserved for fellow police officers who'd done him proud.

Mom just hugged him as I had. "Thank you," she whispered before she embraced me again, Petunia squished between us, and sobbed once. When she pulled away she touched my hair, tears on her red cheeks. "You look a fright, sweetie," she said with one of her patented forced, everything's going to be fine, Lucy Fleming smiles. "Let's get you cleaned up."

Dad hesitated. "I can find Ava?"

I shook my head, managed a smile at last. I was safe. It was going to be all right. And the person who killed Mason—who tried to kill me—was in for a hell of a ride when I finally found them.

"I just need a minute," I said, letting Mom lead me away, needing in that moment for my mother to take care of me, even if only for a little while.

We headed back to my room, this time Mom taking the elevator and me without the energy to talk her out of it. I honestly don't think I would have made it up seven flights anyway, so if the elevator did die and we were trapped in there? So be it. I set Petunia down as soon as we exited into the corridor, arms shaking from the effort to hold her but loathe to release her. She trotted beside me, looking up at me. Was that worry in her bulging eyes? Did she sense I had been in trouble? I fished out my key—thank goodness I hadn't lost it in the snow, too—and let Mom go first, the pug sticking with me like glue.

A change of clothes and washing my face helped restore me somewhat, as did the shot of whiskey Mom handed me when I emerged from the bathroom in jeans and a fluffy sweater, updo ravaged by the storm now wound into a messy bun at the base of my neck. Looked like trash, but the best I could do.

"Drink it," Mom said, practically holding it to my lips, Dad's flask in her other hand.

I tipped it without argument, the heat crawling down my throat and making me cough. But the last edges of my terror vanished and I took one last swig for good measure.

"You're sure you're all right?" Mom's face fell for an instant and I just kissed her cheek.

"About angry enough to tear this place apart looking for the killer," I said.

She smiled, wavering, tremulous. "Are you sure?" I should have expected that from Mom, and likely from Dad, too. And when my father filled him in, Crew. Damn it, the killer might not have succeeded in eliminating me through murder but they might have thanks to the protective natures of the ones I had to answer to.

"Mom," I said, grasping her upper arms in my hands and shaking her ever so slightly. "You taught me to never be afraid. Not of anything." She nodded, though it seemed like she didn't want to but couldn't help herself. "So I'm going back out there," I said, "and I'm going to finish what I started because no one does that to a Fleming and gets away with it."

Maybe if I'd tried another argument I would have lost. Instead, the pride that flared in her eyes immediately preceded a massive hug so enthusiastic Petunia howled softly and bounced on her back legs to paw at us for attention. "That's my girl," Mom whispered in my ear before letting me go. She looked down at Petunia, I'm sure to try to hide the tears she blinked away, grinning at the dog. "Right, darling pug? That murderer can just watch out."

Now, to convince Dad and the sheriff before they locked me in my room and threw away the key.

I guess I shouldn't have been surprised to encounter Crew the second Mom and I returned to the lobby. He stood with Dad and Bill, the two older men hanging back as the sheriff almost leaped on me, examining me as if for damage while I gaped at him like he'd lost his mind.

"You're not hurt?" He cleared his throat and backed off and I wondered for a minute if Vivian liked stewing alone in her room while I spent so much time with her date. Sucker.

"I'm okay," I said, smiling at the maintenance man lingering with Dad. "Thanks to Bill and Moose."

But, as I expected, Crew had ideas about whether I was actually okay or not and it was clear from the way he shook his head, from that flat and distant expression he acquired, he'd made up his mind about my future involvement. No surprise there. "That's it," he said, hardly a shocker, "you're done, Fee. Go to your room right now and stay out of it."

Mom was on my side, I knew that. I'd won her over, but I hadn't had a chance to talk to my father. And so, when Crew delivered his ultimatum, I fully expected my ex-sheriff and overly protective dad to take Crew's side. Which meant a giant battle I didn't have the energy to fight.

Instead of adding his own stern command to Crew's, however, Dad shocked me. I don't know who laughed harder, Mom or my normally stoic father. To hear them, they might as well have been a pair of cackling hyenas. Mom's turned to giggles while Dad wiped at his eyes and clasped one hand to Crew's shoulder.

"Good luck telling a Fleming woman what to do," he said, winking at me. And told me with that wink he'd already come to his own conclusions about what I was capable of and had no plans to hold me back.

Wow. Who was this man and what did he do with my dad?

Crew's forehead vein made an appearance, the left eye twitch of doom making him look slightly demented. But when he sighed and shrugged and met my gaze again, I could tell he'd given up all hope of success and was just going to ride the wave until he could be rid of me when the storm was over.

I'd take it.

"If you don't mind," Bill said, nodding to us, "I have rounds to make. And I have to top up the fuel in the gennies. Bosses will be at me if I let the power go out."

"Thank you and hug Moose for me." I bent and scooped up Petunia, hugging her tight a moment before she grunted loudly enough I set her down.

Her butt found my toes and we were happy all over again.

"Okay, let's lay this out then," Dad said. "Shall we?" He gestured at Crew. "What have you got, Sheriff?"

"Ethan," he said immediately. "He's the most logical choice, means, motive and tons of opportunity." Crew shook his head then. "Without any forensics, though, it's impossible to know for sure. But he's my number one."

"Agreed," Dad said. "I liked Simone for this—no offence, kid," he waved off my protest, "until Ethan's story came out. Still, the brother's a bit of a screw up and money's a motivator. So Noah?"

"Bottom of the list if he's even on it." Mom shocked me with her offering. "I like James Adler for this." Mom punctuated her opinion with a sniff. "If I thought that little monster was connected to the death of my daughter he wouldn't make it twenty-four hours." We all gaped at her while she arched an eyebrow. "What?"

"Flemings," Crew said like that was a bad thing.

"There's one person we're not considering," I said slowly, hesitating.

"I've already cleared the chef and the stepfather," Crew said. "And the general manager, the rest of the staff."

That was fast for him. From the way Dad grinned, though, it was apparent they'd had another chat and my father must have won, at least in this instance. Enough to keep Dad in a good mood and tweak Crew to the point of frustration. These two had to sit down and have a serious conversation about how they were going to exist together before something bigger crawled out of the woodwork.

My mind let that go in favor of this particular mess. "You know Carol and Lucas are an item, yes?" Crew hesitated which meant he hadn't known but now he did. Good for him. "But I agree. None of the others are good for this. Look." I reached for my phone and groaned. "Damn it. I lost my phone in the snow when... you know."

"Here." Crew handed me his. Why wasn't I surprised at the gigantic, rubberized safety box he had around his latest and greatest in smartphone tech? If I was right, he could drop this baby in the ocean and it would still work a week later. But it wasn't the phone itself that gave me a thrill of surprise. The fact he just handed it over felt oddly intimate. "What are you looking for?"

I opened his social media to which he grunted and perhaps realized his mistake. I flinched briefly at the selfie of him and Vivian from earlier tonight, though part of me acknowledged the discomfort in his face and the overly eager smile on hers before I keyed in Mason's name and found his profile. Wide open and completely viewable. I located one of the party picture folders and showed it to Crew, paging through a few images for him before he got the hint. And looked up at the same moment Dad did from watching over his shoulder while Mom squinted and asked the question the boys were rolling over in their heads.

"Who's that in the background?" Clever Mamma Fleming. She wasn't a sheriff's wife for nothing. I wondered how many cases she helped Dad solve on the down low all those years. She was certainly showing her investigative savvy now. "She's in every photo."

"That," I said with a quiver in my stomach and the refusal to believe a ghost had tried to kill me, "is Elizabeth Adler." I paused. "I think."

Crew flipped through again while Mom shook her head with a sorrowful expression. But I didn't get to tell them where my head was, because a soft voice interrupted and turned me around.

"Miss Fleming? Fee?" Ava stood there, looking anxious and raising both hands to Crew who instantly scowled in her direction. "I know, I'm sorry. I'm going back to my room. But Simone wanted to see Fee. Is that okay?"

"Of course it is." I linked arms with her, Petunia following at my heels, and left with the young ski instructor, leaving my suppositions about the ghost of Elizabeth Adler for now, still not convinced I had things right away. And I'd been wanting to talk to Ava alone anyway and this was the perfect opportunity to escape any chance Crew or Dad or even Mom might change their minds about locking me up for my own safety. I could tell, when I glanced back, all three of the people I'd just left weren't happy with me just wandering off like this, and I actually felt touched. But I was pretty positive it wasn't Ava who tried to kill me and I really did need to get her alone.

Turned out the feeling was mutual. Instead of leading me to the staff quarters as I'd expected, Ava tugged me into the women's washroom and leaned against the door, Petunia's claws clicking on the tile while she sat to watch us talk.

"I'm sorry," Ava said, a bit breathless. "I didn't mean to lie just now but I really wanted to talk to you."

"Simone's not looking for me," I said.

"Well, she kind of is, but not really." Ava bit her lower lip and tugged at the hem of her white staff golf shirt. She'd changed as I had, now the alluring ski instructor with the big eyes and bouncing pony of thick hair, all innocence and youthful sunshine. Except it was clear she was deeply troubled. "I just, I had to tell you and I didn't want to betray him to them, not unless you thought I was right." She tossed her hands, clearly flustered. "I feel horrible doing this, but Fee, I think Noah was right and Ethan killed Mason."

"Why?" And why now this confession?

"Because," she whispered, "I wasn't going to Colorado or New Zealand and Ethan knew it before we even came here."

CHAPTER TWENTY-THREE

THAT WAS A GUILTY verdict if ever I heard one. "You told him you weren't going?"

She swallowed hard. "Well, no," she said. "I told Mason I wasn't. He said he was going to tell Ethan. That was a week ago so I assume he did."

Smoking gun not so smoking. "Ava, were you in love with Mason?"

She shook her head with enough violence her hair shivered around her, pieces coming loose from the ponytail to cling to her neck in static charged strands. The look of horror on her face told me the thought never crossed her mind before she could gasp her audible denial. "No! No." Ava hugged herself, rubbing her upper arms with both hands, looking down at her feet a moment before meeting my gaze with hers. She was barely five feet, tiny but muscular from the way her forearms corded when she squared her shoulders and jutted her chin like she expected to be judged. "I'm asexual," she said with the kind of firmness that told me she was still learning how to express it to people without feeling awkward. "I don't even feel that way about Ethan." Now she blushed for real, but didn't avert her eyes. "He knows," she said. "I told him. He doesn't care. But that's the thing, I do." She dropped her hands, stuffed them in her back pockets, distress clear. "He deserves someone who can love him and give him what he wants. I can't. And I don't want to, either. I don't want to be someone I'm not."

Five years in New York had introduced me to the fact there were many kinds of people in many kinds of situations who lived happy and interesting lives nothing at all like mine. And though maybe I didn't understand completely those lives, I fully accepted them because mine wasn't all that hot, was it? Who was I to judge? So Ava's sexual identity wasn't my business, unless it added to Ethan's motive. I nodded encouragement while she drew a breath and when she went on it was in a much calmer and less defensive state.

"Most people ask me if I'm sure," she said softly. "Tell me I'm too pretty to be deviant like that."

"Most people are assholes," I said, and she giggled, the last of her tension about her admission gone, if returned as she sighed out her amusement.

"When it came to Mason and the lodge, I was staying for the money, plain and simple." She wrinkled her turned up nose and laughed then, a barking sound of practicality and joylessness. "Ethan's really a great skier and an amazing teacher. But I've been told I could be on the national snowboarding team. And I really, really want the chance to try out."

Ah. "And Ethan doesn't want you to?"

"He doesn't think it's practical," she said like she was repeating him word for word and tone for tone, looking away at last, voice dropping like she believed him once and still fought her demons over her own talent. "The chance to try, though." When she looked up once more joy and excitement blazed in her gaze. "I was going to spend the winter here and work on my skills, then meet Ethan in New Zealand—or go alone, if I could connect with someone on the team who was going and tag along with them. Mason said he could hook me up if that was what I wanted when the season ended." Her face crumpled briefly. "Now I don't know what I'm going to do. That's so selfish of me, but I can't help feeling like I've lost so much in this."

Honestly, I didn't blame her that feeling of loss. Not for Mason but her future. I'd been there and not so long ago, thanks to Ryan and his cheating. If it hadn't been for Grandmother Iris's death and my inheritance of Petunia's, would I still be in New York trying to find my way and losing myself all over again? But this wasn't about me.

"Bill Saunders seems to think Mason had some good in him," I said.

She shrugged, laughed. "I don't know, Fee. Maybe. There were moments I got to see him, the real him, you know? Deep down, that hurt boy who just wanted people to like him. Who just wanted to trust. And then bam, he'd be this total and utter asshole who did everything he could to hurt you and laughed when he did it. Thought crushing your soul was funny."

"But he was helping you?"

"Only because of that night," she said. "When I saved his life. Things changed between us. I wasn't just Ethan's girlfriend anymore, another cute blonde who could snowboard. I was Ava to him all of a sudden and he took the people he noticed very seriously."

"Including Simone?" I needed to know she really was in the clear and Ava would know. Bad friend.

Ava's face fell and she hesitated before sighing. "No offense to Simone," she said. "I really like her and she's a great person. But Mason was just using her like he did every other girl."

"Every other girl but you." I waited for Ava to answer but she didn't get the chance.

Not when a stall door slammed open and a statuesque black girl dove for Ava, plowing into her and carrying her to the ground with a shriek like a battle cry. Petunia burst into aggressive barking, something she never did, backing away with her black ears back and the line of fur along her spine standing up

I leaped into the fight before it could really get started, jerking Simone free of Ava who sobbed as she crouched on the tile, her arms covering her face. Simone, on the other hand, shook and snarled, her hands curving into claws with those very sharp nails likely able to leave serious injury if she was allowed to get a good slap in.

"Let me go!" She jerked against me but I held on tight, had enough experience with self-defense and her sister's occasional drunken rampages I knew what I was capable of, and what she could do, too. Simone sagged against me while Ava slowly climbed to her feet and, misery written all over her, met the other girl's eyes.

"I'm so sorry," she breathed while Simone snapped at her.

"You're not sorry," she screeched, making my head ache from the volume. "You wanted Mason to yourself all along. I bet you dosed him at his party last year so you could save him and get his attention." Simone was sobbing now, and so was Ava, two weeping girls a bit more than I could handle in my present weakened state. While the initial adrenaline had given me the power I needed to pull Simone off, I was quickly running down my meter and any second now I'd have to sit down or I'd fall down.

"You heard our whole conversation," I said, knowing reasonable likely wouldn't reach Simone at the moment but trying anyway. "You know that's not true."

"I just wanted to help." Ava was back to hugging herself, ignoring her own tears. I eased up on Simone who showed no further sign of physically assaulting the smaller girl so I left them both long enough to duck into one of the pink painted stalls and retrieve a hand full of toilet paper, pausing to soothe Petunia with a pat. The wad split between them, I heaved myself up on the counter and leaned against the mirror behind me, my pug clicking forward to sit between my feet, while I hoped the girls didn't see just how weak I was even as spots danced in my vision.

Simone sat on the floor, long legs curling beneath her, sparkling gown puddled around her. Ava joined her and tentatively took her hand. The taller girl hugged her suddenly and the pair broke down into sobbing apologies for each other while I sighed and closed my eyes in relief.

When I opened them again, the two were still holding hands and talking and had Petunia between them, the pug curled up and enjoying their absent pats as they chatted. Had I passed out for a second?

Possibly. But I woke up again at the good part, apparently.

"I just want to go home," Simone said. "This is a disaster. I knew better, A. You told me this was a terrible idea."

"The heart wants what it wants," Ava said with a sad smile. "And for all I knew you were the one for him. You had to try."

"You're just being kind, now and I don't deserve that." Simone heaved a big sigh, smiled up at me through some fresh but cleansing tears. "I threw myself at him like all the other idiot girls at school and he only noticed me because he needed a new conquest. And I gave him that for my moment in the sun." She turned back to Ava and kissed her cheek ever so gently. "He was a dick and a racist and I let him be cruel to people around me because I just needed him to validate me. Imagine that. My sister will kick my ass for being such a jerk."

"Your sister," I said, "doesn't have a leg to stand on in that department, so if she tries you call me and I'll share some stories that will shut her up."

Simone smiled at me before turning back to Ava. "You're the only one who he chased and who turned him down. That's why I was jealous."

"And now you know why." Ava winced. "Will you keep my secret?"

Simone patted her hand. "Girl, you are who you are and there's no shame in it. But I won't tell anyone, I swear."

"You two," I said, "promise me you'll stop fighting and I'll let you go unsupervised."

They helped each other to their feet, Petunia protesting her loss of devoted slaves with a grunt and a soft whine. Ava hesitated, looking down at her, then shrugged as she met my eyes with her own resigned.

"You'll tell the sheriff about me?" A question she assumed she knew the answer to.

"Is your sexual orientation relevant to Mason's murder?" Not to be blunt, but she had to stop fearing who she was.

"No," she said instantly. "At least, I don't think so."

I wasn't sure, especially if Ethan was the murderer. But I'd hold off for the time being until I had to make that choice. "If it's necessary," I said. "Only then."

Ava smiled at me and nodded. "Thank you, Fee," she said.

I thought about hopping down but as they prepared to leave the idea of just sitting here and letting sleep take me became more and more appealing. But Simone was frowning suddenly and came to me and squinted, worry on her face. Ava too as they finally noticed something wasn't right.

"Fee, are you okay?" Simone's hand brushed my cheek, nails scratching gently over the surface. "You look pale."

"Did something happen?" Ava grasped my hand, looked down at it. "Your skin looks like you've been in the cold too long."

Of course she'd recognize that. I pulled away and gave in to moving again, slipped slowly down, smiling at both of them to hide my groan as Petunia came to sit on my feet. "I'm fine," I said. "Thanks for asking." I paused a moment, something niggling. "You said all the girls chased him. Including Elizabeth?"

They groaned together, but in sorrow not judgment.

"Especially Elizabeth," Simone said. "Poor dear."

"Why poor?" I already knew the answer, or guessed it. I'd been to college. Ava's sadness and Simone's sympathy told me I was right.

"I honestly believe he invited her up that mountain to teach her a lesson," Ava said. "He wasn't someone any girl should be chasing."

"Do you think he hurt her?" I wouldn't put it past him. And yet, Bill. Did Mason have murder in him?

Simone hesitated but Ava didn't.

"I think whatever happened to Elizabeth Adler," she said, "Mason wasn't broken up about it."

CHAPTER TWENTY-FOUR

I SENT THE GIRLS on their way back to Ava's quarters, not wanting Simone to be alone in her room upstairs. At least they left as friends and I hoped this brought them closer together. From the way they exited the bathroom with their arms around each other's waists they'd been good buddies all along. Letting a guy come between them? Tragedy.

I stood in the hallway for a moment, thinking, Petunia panting and waiting for me to figure out what I was going to do next. I considered bending to pet her but reconsidered. Wouldn't do to pass out at the moment. Instead, I reached for my phone in my back pocket and swore softly to myself. The odds of finding it before spring were pretty slim and even then it would be dead to the world. But I didn't really care about that part. I'd only had it a short time and just backed up my photos. And my old phone was home with all my contacts intact. No, it was the ease of information access I missed.

Wait, Paisley. She'd told me the Wi-Fi was back up. I headed her way, Petunia chuffing at me as if to say she was a bit tired of all the walking around and couldn't we just stop and lie down already? I ignored her, promising myself I'd take her upstairs shortly and let her sleep. Just as soon as I had another look at Mason's social media.

The front desk stood empty when I strode across the foyer. Maybe Paisley had finally taken a break, poor thing. It had to be close to dawn by now and everyone not involved hopefully tucked in for the night. I know I nearly cracked my jaw with a yawn as I reached the counter, but I had an almost died not so long ago excuse under my belt.

"Hello?" I peeked over the counter. And gasped at the sight of Paisley on the floor. I was already running around the corner and into the office, Petunia huffing after me, when I realized the girl wasn't hurt. My heart tried to leap from my chest regardless, more adrenaline the last thing I needed.

She looked up as Petunia licked her face, squinting with one eye, the other watering.

"Lost my contact," she said, stopping to pat my dog with the softest, kindest expression ever. Petunia had that effect on a lot of people, I noticed. I wasn't the only sucker.

"Ah!" I dove for the floor to help, forgetting my weakness and fighting the black spots that appeared until I slowed down. "Fear not. I've retrieved enough for friends at bars I've become a bit of a contact lens whisperer." She snorted while I slowed my breathing to settle my dizzy spell and skimmed my gaze over the carpet while she struggled to see with one eye. "There!" The little disk of plastic appeared, stuck to the metal side of the filing cabinet by the door. I quickly seized her bottle of solution and squirted some in my palm before gently depositing the drying lens into the puddle to soak. The center was the prettiest shade of brown with little flecks of amber in it. Funny how people liked to augment their eyes— Vivian French's fake piercing blues case in point. I guess I was lucky to have the kind of clear green most of my friends needed contacts to achieve. Instead of commenting, I handed it triumphantly back and grinned.

"One lens rescued."

Paisley exhaled with a big sigh, taking it from me on her now wet fingers after squirting them to clean them before inserting the lens and blinking a few times. She turned back to me once it had settled, cheeks flushed.

"I'm so embarrassed," she said. "That never happens."

"You're lucky if it doesn't," I said. "I have one friend who can't keep hers in. Something to do with the shape of her eye." True story. Mahoney had to give up on them and go back to glasses. And with pupils too big for laser surgery she was stuck and not happy about it even a little.

"Thank you for the help," Paisley said before her face shifted to concern and she reached out to touch my elbow. "I heard you had a fright. Are you okay?"

I'd almost forgotten about my close encounter though I was fairly sure it would be the source of nightmares for me over the next decade or so. "I'm fine," I said, realizing I was lying and that if I didn't find a way to get some rest soon I'd fall over. "Just tired." Yeah, just. "I'm here to ask a favor."

"Anything," she said promptly. "What can I do?"

"You said the internet was back up in here?" I glanced at the computer on the desk nearby. "Do you mind?"

"Not at all." She gestured for me to take a seat. "Is there anything I can help you find?"

It was a huge effort to get up and move, but I did it, shaking my head, sinking into the padded office chair while Petunia settled in her favorite place between my feet. So comforting having her there, while I had a horrible thought. What if she'd been with me when I was pushed out into the storm? I couldn't dream of losing her. Though if Petunia had been there, I doubted the killer would have snuck up on me so successfully. When we got home my pug was getting a treat of epic ice cream proportions. I realized then I was lost in thought and shook myself out of it. "Just checking into something," I said to Paisley, wondering if the smile I wore looked as dazed as it felt, "and needed a bigger monitor." That actually hadn't been true but now that I stared at the twenty inch screen I realized the benefit. So much easier to compare the pictures of Elizabeth to that of the lurker in Mason's photos. Especially in my wobbly condition.

"Do you mind if I sit?" I turned to find her looking out into the empty lobby. "I won't be any trouble."

"Not at all," I said. "Your feet must be killing you. No one to spell your shift?"

She smiled then, quick and perky. "Nancy, our other clerk, made it home before the worst hit. She has a baby and couldn't stay."

"And your manager? Donna Walker, right?"

"She's been in meetings with Mr. Day, Mr. Adler and Chef for the last little while." Not a trace of complaint in her voice. "There's not really much to do, so I'm fine."

"Where are you from, Paisley?" Chit chat wouldn't do me any harm while I did my research and would keep me awake, at least.

"New York," she said promptly.

"City?" I turned and smiled when she nodded . "I was there five years. Quite the town."

"I like it here," she said, voice low and quiet. Almost regretfully. She cleared her throat then. "The lodge is a great place to work and Reading is a nice change from the big city."

"It's a change, that's for sure." I squinted at the images of Mason and the parties, trying for a better look at the lurker, but even with the bigger screen it was hard to see details thanks to flash and focus issues.

"Is that Mason, Mr. Patterson?" Paisley sounded sad.

"His social media," I said. "I'm trying to identify someone in his life. A lurker who seems to be in all his photos."

"Who is it?" Her voice had dropped to a bare whisper as if she were fascinated.

"I don't know," I said, sitting back with a frown. "That's the problem."

"Surely the people he cared about are easy to pick out?" She came to my side and sat in the other office chair, pointing out the usual suspects. "Ethan, Noah, Ava, Simone?"

"It's this person," I said, pointing at the girl in the background. "Have you seen her around here?"

Paisley didn't answer, squinting too before leaning away. "Maybe. I don't know." She shook her head then, met my eyes. "I don't think so."

"I think it might be Elizabeth Adler," I said. "If so, I'm chasing a ghost."

She started like I was serious before her shock turned to a small smile.

"Some ghosts need chasing, I guess," she said. And hesitated. "I heard about her. We all know, because of the staff. It went around to everyone. That he might have hurt that girl. Mr. Adler's daughter."

I nodded. "Well, if he did," I said, "he's paid for it, hasn't he?"

She shrugged. "What a horrible way to die."

Whether she was talking about Elizabeth or Mason or both I had no idea. Even while the lingering question remained—did Elizabeth really die on that mountain? Or did she find a way to get revenge on Mason, possibly with her father's help?

Only one way to find out.

CHAPTER TWENTY-FIVE

Y SEARCH FOR JAMES Adler was quickly curtailed by the huddle of people who caught my attention near the door to the dining room. Crew had been holding his interviews there, rather a bulky location, but I understood his motives. The scene of the crime, while protected as much as it was getting, not to mention the body laid out on the stage, was great incentive to make people talk. And the giant, empty room had to feel oppressive with the looming sheriff standing over you asking very pointed questions while you felt more and more guilty as the seconds ticked by.

Yes, I'd been interrogated by him and knew his tactics. And though they didn't work on me thanks to being raised by a man who perfected said tactics long before I was born and taught them to me whether he planned to or not and my newly discovered talent to ignore blah blah blah thanks to my ex, Ryan, I hadn't felt the pressure of being questioned by Crew Turner. But yes, most certainly, I understood it. And his reasons for it.

Thing was, Crew might have been a budding expert—or a master for all I knew—compared to my dad and whether my father believed in that technique under these circumstances or not. But the woman who stood with her shoulders back and her shining hair tossing as she delivered whatever it was she was saying? She'd achieve the rank of super empress of do it now and don't you dare backtalk.

Olivia Walker's tirade was easy enough to guess at and my mind filled in the blanks pretty quickly when I closed the gap, pug in pursuit, and caught the thread of the conversation. No, not convo. Tyrannical oration.

"—clean up this mess in the next sixty minutes, I'll have your job, Crew Turner. And don't think that means for one moment you're off the hook for this disaster, John. Both of you have fumbled this investigation from the get go and I've spent the last several hours not only calming my guests but assuring our visiting funders that this town of ours isn't some kind of cesspool of murder and dark secrets!" Except from what I'd seen so far, it was. At least two murders in eight months and a whole lot of covering up to do in the meantime? How much had she done to distract from the shoddy building practices of one Pete Wilkins? I was pretty sure if it weren't for Jared being a good guy and owning up to his father's illegal and unethical practices, this lodge would likely be condemned for structural issues.

While the two sheriffs, past and present, looked hangdog and did their best to mumble their apologies, I stepped into the circle—pug immediately sitting on my feet in her delight at stopping—and observed the true mistress of all things awesome in action.

Olivia might have been mayor, but she held zero candles to the power of my family's matriarch. Mom, her green eyes shining and a brilliantly constructed smile on her face, used her very best teacher voice as she tilted that red head and unleashed the Fleming all over our dear mayor's ass.

"Dear Olivia," she said, "while I voted for you and I'm happy I did so, let me tell you in no uncertain terms if you don't ease up for five minutes you're going to die of a self-inflicted aneurysm." Olivia gaped at her while Mom forged on in the nicest possible way. "Now, let me tell you what's going to happen from here. You are going to go back to the investors and tell them everything is under control." She stepped close to Olivia, cutting through the circle and hooking her hand through the mayor's arm. "And I'm going to join you. Together, we're going to make sure those lovely ladies and gentlemen and their development money are happy to stay in Reading while the three people I trust most to handle this little stumbling block find the answers we need."

Olivia tried to resist, but she obviously didn't know Mom like I knew Mom. "They're going to run like rabbits." Was that a wail in the back of her voice? "All my hard work, Lu."

"It's fine," Mom said with a pish-tosh kind of snort. "Let's stop at the bar and pick up some liquor. That'll take care of everything."

"You really think so?" Poor Olivia was clearly exhausted. How long had she been working on tonight? I'd seen the barest signs of strain in her even when she'd come to Petunia's to order me to attend. Surely she'd worn herself thin before the night even got started. Instead of fighting, clearly at the brink of her energy, she let Mom lead her away.

"I know so." My mother waved at us and hustled to the bar with the mayor in tow while I giggled behind my hands and Petunia farted with great enthusiasm.

"Your mother," Crew said, then laughed.

"Your mother," Dad said. Snorted.

"My mother," I finished for them with a big grin, "needs to run for mayor."

The three of us broke into weary laughter. It really wasn't that funny except we were all tired and humor seemed the cure to our ills. I sobered at last, the two sheriffs joining me, though the mood had lightened somewhat and I felt, for the first time ever, like I belonged in this little circle with them.

Funny how that happened.

"Don't put that idea in Lu's head, please," Dad said then with a wink. "Bad enough she bosses me around."

"Yes," Crew groaned. "Please. Olivia's hard enough to deal with. But I'd never be able to say no to Lucy. She's too…"

"Fleming," Dad and I said together. More giggles. That felt good.

Mom reappeared, Olivia hurrying across the foyer from the bar toward the elevators with her arms full of bottles. My mother's rapid approach told me she was on a mission and the look on her face said she was out of patience at last.

How did I know? Because Lucy Fleming looked annoyed and Mom never, ever showed it when she was pissed.

"You three." She stopped and stabbed an index finger at us. "Whatever I said to Olivia, forget it." Wow, Mom. "I'll do what I can to keep her off your back, you're welcome." I would have sniggered except I was pretty sure any sign of amusement would have set her off. I'd never seen her like this before. "But you'd better get to it. Your murderer? Literally trapped here. It can't be that hard to find a killer when that killer can't leave."

"Lu—"

Dad. Oh, Dad. Shut up.

"Johnathan Albert Campbell Fleming." She'd pulled out all four names. Not good. "My feet hurt. I'm tired and hungry and I didn't get my cake." Why did she sound most put out by that last fact? "And

I'm willingly about to spend the next hour or so with Olivia Walker appeasing her silly funders with a smile on my face. The least you can do is find one little murderer. Get cracking." With that, she spun on her heel and marched off to Olivia, taking some of the bottles from her, punching the number to the penthouse. The two stepped on the elevator without another look our way and I waited until the doors closed to punch Dad in the arm with a snorting giggle that turned into a near breathless he-haw.

"Dad," I said, trying to breathe. "What is wrong with you?"

"Just a little murderer," he muttered while Crew shook his hand with a solid nod.

"I envy your courage," he said with utmost sincerity before cracking a grin. "I've known her one short year and I wouldn't try to talk back to your wife."

Dad grimaced. "Okay, very funny. Knock it off and let's focus."

"Just one little murderer," Crew said. And laughed.

That set us all off again but when we pulled ourselves together at last, I sighed and shrugged.

"We're back where we started," I said. "I have no idea who tried to kill me, though I'm pretty sure it was our little murderer." Wasn't so funny now.

"At least that means your mother's right," Crew said. "And the killer didn't escape before the storm. So we do have time."

"Ava and Simone are out of the picture," I said and then filled them in on the scene in the bathroom, leaving out Ava's confession about her personal life. "Ethan may or may not have known she was staying, depending on how cruel Mason was feeling."

Crew nodded. "So as Bill Saunders and Carol Chaney as far as I'm concerned. If the chef wanted to kill Mason why do it in a way that points right to her? And the maintenance man was here thanks to Mason."

Dad grunted. "Really, our only solid suspects remaining are Ethan Perry—"

"And James Adler." I finished for him. I hated to think Elizabeth's father had anything to do with it. Surely he'd lost enough when he lost her.

"Agreed," Crew said. "One long, last chat with Mr. Adler and then we lock the two of them up until my forensics team can get here. Or until one of them confesses."

Yeah, like that was going to happen.

CHAPTER TWENTY-SIX

S O STRANGE TO BE part of the team, the portly pug my constant companion as I joined Dad and Crew in the dining room and wasn't being glared at for interfering or anything. It would have been rather exciting if I cared about such things. Which I didn't. Yeah, okay then.

Crew led the interrogation though, of course and I couldn't help but wonder how Dad felt about that. The blank mask my father wore hid most things from the world, though I could often see past his deadpan stare into the little tells that showed what he was really thinking and feeling. I'd spent enough time with him as a small girl—my best friend growing up—his grumbling grumpiness never intimidated me.

Not that Dad was open about his feelings or anything. Heaven forbid John Fleming showed a hint of weakness, tough old-school sheriff that he was. But I saw past his bluster enough times it was usually easy to read him.

Not tonight, though. Wait, this morning, right? It was now past 3AM if the clock in the office was correct and hadn't been accidentally reset by the loss of power. Maybe I was just tired, but Dad's empty expression and stolid stance as he observed Crew gave me nothing.

That could have meant there was nothing to see. Though I doubted it.

James Adler, on the other hand, was a fount of emotions, probably because he'd imbibed enough alcohol between the last time I'd talked to him and now that from the smell of him he'd turned his insides permanently liquid. It was possible Lucas Day's business partner thought he was doing a great job of hiding how he felt, but with every question Crew asked his face twisted, his words slurring through a range of volume and timber while I alternated between sympathy for him and the kind of hysterical amusement that came with over exhaustion.

"They never found Elizabeth's body, then, is that what you're telling me?" Crew had to start with the man's loss, didn't he? Okay, no judging, because Dad likely would have, too. If this was my interrogation I would have gotten there eventually and in a way that soothed the poor man's grief.

James's eyelids flickered, entire expression turning downward while he reached for a glass that had been empty the last three times he tried to drink from it. He stared down into the last drops of amber whiskey as he answered, just this side of plastered so he was coherent, but not by much.

"Call the cops in Aspen," he said, heart in his voice, "they'll tell you everything."

"They aren't here," Crew said without a hint of compassion while I tsked beside him. He threw me one of those looks I was getting used to but chose to ignore and without actually deciding to interrupt, I interrupted. Pulled a chair over beside James and relieved him of the glass before holding his big hand between mine.

"Mr. Adler," I said with as much kindness as I could muster, Petunia standing on her back legs to push her head under his hand. He automatically stroked her wrinkled noggin while I went on, the soothing presence of my dog a boon as always. "I know how hard this is. That Mason's death is stirring up things you would rather remain buried."

"I didn't get to bury her." James broke down into tears at my choice of words, leaning forward and I hugged him while Petunia sank to her haunches and whined sympathetically. His forehead rested on my shoulder while I glared at Crew and he glared back at me. There it was, the expected reaction from the sheriff. Now I could carry on.

"I'm so sorry," I said, patting the weeping man's shoulder, choking a bit on the fumes from the whiskey on his breath. There was no way he drank as much as he had if this wasn't a regular thing for him, because a normal person with a typical routine wouldn't have been able to stomach so much. Another sign of his suffering. "Can you tell us what happened? It's important, maybe more important than you know."

James sat back, nodded, snuffling. I handed him one of the napkins left discarded on the table behind me and he used it liberally on his face, though after he was done he cleared his throat and somehow pulled himself together enough when he met my eyes his weren't as unfocused as they had been.

"I miss her so much," he whispered, coughed softly. "Her mother died when she was just a little girl and Elizabeth was all I had. She was never the prettiest or the smartest or the bravest. But she was my daughter." I feared he might devolve into weeping again but held his composure past the short, deep sob that followed his last word then went on. "I didn't want her hanging out with Mason and his friends. They were so cruel to her and she refused to see it. But *I* saw it." He jabbed a finger at the body under the sheet twenty feet away. "I watched him abuse her and treat her like garbage and laugh about it. Him and his pathetic unfriends."

"She just wanted to fit in." I nodded and squeezed his hand still in my grasp. "It's hard when you're that age, trying to find your way."

"She could have had lots of friends," James said, sagging. "So many wonderful people out there. But she chose to chase that worthless piece of trash. And I couldn't convince her otherwise."

Yeah, no animosity there, then, right?

"Mr. Adler." Dad's tone matched mine while Crew huffed softly under his breath. In protest? Well, considering I'd gotten more out of James in the last minute or so than he had in the previous ten Crew had been questioning the man, he could just hold his freaking horses already. "What happened that day?"

"Elizabeth didn't make that cake," James said, like it meant something. Of course she didn't. Carol did. She told me as much.

And then, in a flash, everything made sense. And my annoyance with Simone and Ava made me want to stomp off to give the pair of them hell for not telling me what I now understood. "Mason thought Elizabeth baked the cake that almost killed him last year." Whatever misplaced loyalty the girls felt, whatever their reasoning for holding back Mason's blame about the cake, it was an important piece of information I could have used going into this little chat instead of sitting there, gaping at Elizabeth's father and at a loss for words.

But, apparently that stunned silence worked to my advantage. James nodded, wiping at his eyes randomly with the napkin. "He blamed her for it, but it wasn't her. He refused to believe her. And if Marie was still alive, I know her family would have tried to sue. But no one would own up to who made it so Elizabeth had that hanging over her head for weeks."

"That's why you think Mason might have hurt her the day they went skiing." I'd have made the same assumption with this tidbit in hand.

"He turned from horrible ass to all sweet and forgiving in a snap." James tried to mimic the word with his thumb and forefinger but his coordination just wasn't there. He frowned at his fingers like he might have a few more visible than he actually owned then shook his head and went on. "I begged her not to go but she was so happy. I'd never seen her smile so bright." He blinked, tears welling once more. "So I relented and I will never, ever forgive myself for that."

"James." I hadn't noticed Lucas's arrival, and from the surprised look on Crew and Dad's faces they hadn't either. "Stop talking. You need a lawyer." The expression on the man's face told me he'd heard everything and suddenly doubted his partner's innocence. About as much as I was doubting. Or maybe not so suddenly?

"Oh, you're coming to my defense now, are you, Lucas?" James's entire attitude shifted as he tried to spin around to confront the other man, wobbling in the chair as he did before turning back to me. "You weren't there for me when they came back without her, though, were you?"

Lucas fell silent, face twisting in a mix of what looked like grief and regret.

"They left after lunch, Elizabeth with them." James's eyes locked on mine and held me tight. "I watched them go, Mason with his arm around her shoulders. She wasn't a strong skier, not at all. But he took her all the way to the last black diamond that day, the one the hill closed because it was too dangerous, the conditions already causing three accidents. Not that he cared. He and his friends skied down that run and left her at the top of the mountain, terrified. At least, that's what he told me when they came back. Last to arrive, alone, five minutes after the others. Said he took a spill and had a cut on his cheek to prove it. But I knew better. They couldn't find her body, didn't see her anywhere."

"So you think he waited for the others to go, attacked her, she got a blow in and he killed her and left her where she wouldn't be found." Was Mason a murderer too for real?

James shrugged, collapsing in on himself as grief and too much whiskey finally defeated the tall, lean man. I watched his outrage and his anger die and leave him a broken shell filled with booze and hate. "At the very least, he left her alone up there. A death sentence for someone who couldn't ski such a treacherous run. And at the most?" He shrugged absently. "At the most, he did something to her. No matter what, she's dead and it's Mason's fault. And thanks to Marie and her money and her family? He got away with murder."

I was partial to the latter. Elizabeth could have backtracked her way to another run, looked for help. Returned to the lift. Unless, that was, she couldn't. Because Mason hurt or killed her.

"There was no proof of that," Lucas said, though his voice cracked when he spoke and it sounded like it was something he practiced saying too many times to be authentic anymore.

James barked the kind of soft laugh that sounded like it hurt. "If I hadn't been neck deep in this project already, I'd have walked away and sued all of you. But everything I have is invested in this lodge. And with Elizabeth gone, it's all I have left."

How utterly horrible and, as I looked up to Crew despite my sympathy for the poor man's hurt, an absolutely ideal motive for murder.

"You knew Mason was allergic." Crew didn't ask.

James nodded. "Everyone did, Marie made damned sure of that, how her precious child was never to be put at risk. That's why I know Elizabeth didn't bake that cake. But Mason wouldn't believe her and he killed her in revenge. I'm sure of it."

"We'll need to know your movements from the time you arrived until Mason died," Crew said.

"Ask Lucas where I was. And that mayor of ours." James tried to stagger to his feet but fell back into the chair again where he sighed deeply like a man who had finally given up. "I was with them the whole time."

"Did you visit the men's washroom in the lobby at any point before Mason's death?" I shushed Crew with a wave of one hand, cutting off his next question with my own. Yeah, that went over well, but the sheriff held his tongue at least while James shook his head and Lucas spoke for him.

"The one in the bar," the victim's stepfather said. "I was with him the entire night."

"Worried about my drinking, aren't you, Lucas?" James's bitterness hadn't left him. "And the last of the money you want for the final payment."

"James, that's not fair." Lucas looked and sounded like a man who truly suffered for his friend.

But James Adler didn't seem to care about what his partner felt. "Tell Elizabeth about fair," he said.

CHAPTER TWENTY-SEVEN

W E LEFT LUCAS SITTING with James, the drunken man now passed out and snoring on his folded arms, the table before him shaking slightly as he snored in his inebriated stupor.

"I'll make sure he's okay," Lucas told us. "I'm sorry about this."

"You do realize he's our number one suspect." Crew didn't pull punches, did he?

But Lucas wasn't surprised while my mind still churned with possibilities. "I worried as much," he said. "And I have to admit when Mason died, it was my first thought." He seemed genuinely troubled by that. "Which makes me exactly the kind of man James thinks I am, I suppose."

I followed Crew and Dad toward the doors to the dining room, keeping up with their long strides, Petunia grunting her complaint we were moving again while Dad said, "Security footage?" and Crew grunted his agreement.

"Wait a second," I said, anger flaring. "You two haven't looked at any of it yet?" What the hell had they been up to all this time? And why hadn't I remembered to check it myself while I was in the office? Yeah, who was I really annoyed with right now?

"We looked at some of it," Crew said with a faint hint of amusement in his voice, enough to rile me up because he was clearly humoring me, the jerk. "But I want to double check that Lucas was with James the whole time."

"The two of them could have worked this out," Dad said in a low voice. "The whole act in there might have been part of the plan to get away with murder."

"I thought of that," Crew grumbled back while I sighed and rolled my eyes at their wide shoulders striding ahead of me and making me and my portly pug run to keep up.

Competitive boy hormones were stupid.

Paisley smiled at us behind the counter as we approached and immediately gestured for us to come around the counter when Crew asked to see the tapes from tonight. I found myself tucked in behind him, feet warmed by dog butt, Dad to one side, as she keyed up the timecode they asked for—just before dinner in the bar area—and nothing happened. No, not nothing specifically. But static, lots of snowy hissing on black. Paisley made a soft sound of protest, frowning as she reentered her command to the digital recorder and got the same thing.

Crew leaned in over her shoulder, squinting at the computer. "You're sure you got the right file?"

She nodded and swallowed, leaning back and sliding out of the chair, gesturing for him to take the seat. "You can look for yourself," she said, face twisting in worry, "but it's gone."

"How much?" I reached out and squeezed her hand in reassurance because if it was me, I'd be making a giant mind leap to being accused of deleting the footage.

"From what I can tell," Paisley said with a swallow and wide eyes, "all of it."

"But it was here not too long ago." Dad crossed his arms over his chest, giving her the Fleming stink eye while I poked him in the ribs.

"Who had access to the files, Paisley?" Crew tapped away at the keyboard while I tugged on her hand and got her attention, drawing a deep breath of my own and watching her mimic me, smiling a little in obvious gratitude as she refocused.

"Anyone, really," she said. "I've been in and out helping guests all night. Mr. Day was in here, Chef, Mr. Adler. The sheriffs. Bill. You." She covered her mouth with her free hand, eyes even wider as she shook her head. "I didn't mean you had anything to do with it."

"I know," I reassured her. "It's okay. So in other words our murderer could easily have slipped in here and deleted the footage and no one would be the wiser."

Paisley's face fell, crumpled really. "I'm so fired," she said.

Crew sighed at last and sat back, hands slapping his thighs. "Like everything else in this investigation," he snarled, "we have to wait for the damned storm to be over to find out what happened."

"The IT guys can recover whatever is left," Dad said. Trying to be comforting, really?

Crew grunted and stood, glaring at Paisley while she clung to my hand and shivered.

"No one else comes in this office without my permission," he said. Far too late for that but the girl nodded quickly, pale enough I worried if he raised his voice again she might pass out.

"She's alone in here, Crew," I shot back. "And has been for hours. A bit of compassion, maybe?"

He spun on me, his weariness clear in his eyes but not a shred of empathy there to back it up. "You could make yourself useful and babysit." He stormed out and around the desk, crossing the foyer in an aggressive stomp before I could tell him where he could shove that piece of crap that sounded too much like an order.

Dad caught my shoulder in one hand and shook his head at me. "He's under a lot of pressure," he said. Then grinned. "You know, there are times I miss being sheriff. And other times…"

"Like now?" I relented, knowing Crew had to be at the breaking point.

"Well, let's just say, I don't envy the kid. He's got a giant crapshoot ahead of him. But once the storm's cleared and the forensic teams can come in, this will all be worked out."

"As long as the murderer doesn't escape before then." I shook my head, letting Paisley's hand go. She tried another wavering smile I read as gratitude. "When the storm breaks, you know whoever did it is going to bolt."

"Not if they are in custody already." Dad left me there with the front desk clerk and strode off. Likely to make sure our two main suspects were under wraps. But I had, as yet, to share my own sneaking suspicion. So, with a quick squeeze for Paisley's hand and a, "Ignore that jerk," bit of support for her, I raced after Dad, my weary pug trailing along behind me.

CHAPTER TWENTY-EIGHT

D AD WAS WAITING FOR me in the foyer and, I discovered, so was Crew. The sheriff had obviously gotten over his childish snit fit because he stood with my father and watched me approach. I slowed my pace so I didn't look like a little girl running after her daddy though I was pretty sure I wasn't fooling anyone when I came to a less than graceful stop beside Dad. Petunia let out a long, frustrated sigh and glared at me before burping her opinion of this whole running around business.

"James and Ethan," Crew said before I could open my mouth to him or to Petunia. "Both need to be confined from this moment on in a safe place they can be monitored until the plows get to us and my team can arrive."

"Just those two?" Dad's initial question even sounded cocky and challenging to me though when Crew's forehead vein pulsed, his eye twitch in clear evidence, my father instead held up both hands and shook his head. "Let's just cover all bases, okay?"

Crew grumbled something about too many bases to cover but shrugged and looked away.

"With the security footage damaged, we've lost our chance to double check alibis," Dad said. Sounded super reasonable to me and Crew didn't argue despite the fact he looked like he wanted to call Dad Captain Obvious. "It might be prudent to corral anyone who had a motive at this point."

"We don't have the manpower," Crew said. "Or a location. And despite the fact I'd love to lock up every single person in this hotel, I can't. Because I don't have cause outside of suspicion. Any evidence I might have isn't usable without forensics."

Dad shrugged. "Just a suggestion."

"Before we lock people up now and apologize later," I said, "and trigger Olivia's death throes for ruining her life and Reading's star rankings, can we consider the fact there might be another suspect we're not addressing?" And winced inwardly. I really had to be tired to speak up, my mouth and brain totally disconnected. "If I was going to kill Mason out in the open like that, it would be stupid to do it without a really solid alibi. And a motive to die for."

"Like?" Crew's skepticism wasn't doing much for my own, though it was enough of a challenge to my ego I forged ahead with the idea that lingered with me the last little while.

"Like everyone assuming I'm dead." I waited for them to scoff, to roll their eyes, to do something, anything, that would make me back off this idea—or chase it down like a cheetah hunting a sweet little baby deer on the savannah. And now I had that image in my head and was clearly losing touch with reality thanks to weakness and exhaustion.

Dad spoke first. "Elizabeth Adler."

The way he said it made my skin crawl and suddenly my weird and wild idea wasn't so weird and wild. Not when Crew hesitated before shaking his head.

"Ethan and James both had motive," I said. "But wouldn't it be absolutely stupid to think you could get away with it under these circumstances? Why pick the obvious method, something everyone knew, in a public place with a clear motive pointing fingers at you?" They didn't comment, just watched me. "Sure, murder isn't always the realm of the intelligent, but think about it. This was planned, not spontaneous."

"Unless Ethan spotted the bottle and had an epiphany moment," Crew said, but not arguing, just speculative.

I shrugged. "Fair enough. But think about this for a second. When Elizabeth disappeared, they assumed she was dead. But they didn't find a body," I said. "And while her father's drunken grief in there was real, he might be protecting her. He could have helped her orchestrate this whole thing after collecting the insurance money for her passing. Because we know he's in financial trouble." The more I talked, the crazier I sounded and yet my instincts told me to keep going.

"Don't you think we have enough suspects that we know are alive and kicking and already in this lodge, Fee?" Crew didn't sound as convinced as his words made out. "Chasing ghosts…"

I sighed, rubbed my forehead with my fingertips. "I just can't get past the cake, the first one. If Elizabeth didn't make it, who did? Who tried to kill Mason that night?"

"James didn't," Dad said. "So does that mean he's not our murderer tonight?"

"That puts the weight all on Ethan," Crew said. "Are we saying that, John?"

Dad didn't answer.

"We're working on the premise that Mason's near death last year was intentional," Crew said. "But what if it really was an accident?"

"Then we're back to square one," I said.

There wasn't much left to say. We parted ways, Dad heading for the staff quarters and Ethan, Crew for James while I slumped my way to the bar, Petunia dragging her butt and ready to crash, in search of a drink for both of us and the means to silence the weird feeling I had we were missing something.

If that was Elizabeth lurking in those photos, maybe James could identify her. If it wasn't, then did we have another suspect after all? One we had as yet to sort out? Whoever killed the power in the hall and tried to condemn me to a snowy grave was strong, but not overly so. I drew a breath as I circled the bar and poured myself two fingers of scotch before topping the glass with another two. Mom had left some of the good stuff behind at least. I hadn't yet let myself linger over the details of the attack, partly out of sheer tiredness and partly out of fear. But I needed to remember because whoever tried to kill me was Mason's murderer, I was sure of it.

"Okay, pug," I said, sitting down and patting the bench seat beside me, helping her up when she decided she couldn't make it on her own, buggy eyes begging for a lift. She settled next to me, a bowl of water slopped over the edges while I talked it through. "I heard rustling, like leaves moving. The lights went out. I didn't hear anything else, I'm sure of it. The exit light went out, too, and the emergency beacon over the staff door. Was I followed? If so, how did the killer know how to shut off the lights in just that area? Because whoever it is works here." Okay then. "Or has access to the place." That didn't eliminate James. Or did it? The man was roaring drunk. And far too tall, I realized. Comparing his height in my head to the feeling of the person who shoved me didn't match. I closed my eyes and let myself remember.

Something hit me hard in the shoulder, driving me sideways and into the double doors at my right. I cried out in surprise as the way parted, a chill wash of snow hitting me, wind buffeting against me while, shock taking over—

I inhaled and shuddered, shaking off the terror of the memory. This was a bad idea to do while I was this tired and worn thin. Just closing my eyes put me on the edge of sleep, a terrible place to linger while I tried to recall almost dying. Still, a detail struck me as I examined the memory again, excitement replacing my fear.

The person who hit me wasn't tall. Certainly not big like James or even Ethan. Their shoulder hit my shoulder, the clear feeling of being struck with another person's upper arm and side embedded in my body memory. Whoever tried to kill me was my height or maybe even a little shorter.

But who did that leave except the ghost of Elizabeth Adler?

I was so lost in this scrap of information I looked up in surprise when someone entered the bar, the tapping of high heels making me jump. I sagged into the cushions of the bench, Petunia wriggling her delight at the sight of Daisy striding toward me still in full party gear. But the look on her face told me she'd had about enough of her own night, thanks and I poured her a stiff glass of her own, sliding it toward her when she halted at the table and lifted it with a graceful catch, sipping it before arching one eyebrow at me.

"You," she said, "look like crap."

"Thanks," I said. "Almost dying will do that to you."

Her annoyed expression flashed to fear and then worry as her jaw dropped, big, gray eyes full of guilt. "Fee, oh my god, what happened? Were you serious just now? Or are you being funny? You don't look like you're being funny."

I filled her in while she sank down beside Petunia, the two of us sharing another quick shot of scotch, the buzz hitting me hard a moment before settling into a mellow kind of warmth I could handle.

"I can't believe you almost died." She gripped my hand in hers, tears standing in her eyes. "I just found you again. I don't know what I'd do if anything happened to you."

I tossed her a napkin with my free hand. "Don't go getting maudlin on me," I said. "I'm okay. Still have all my parts." I wiggled my fingers at her. "But yeah, it was close."

"And you didn't see anyone?" The ridiculousness of who I suspected held me silent while she reacted with disdain for her own question. "Sorry, I'm sure you would have done something if you had." Daisy's face fell. "I'm so stupid all the time." And burst into tears.

I hugged her over the whining body of my pug because that little personal attack on herself wasn't about me almost dying. Or anything like the cheerfully and sometimes painfully optimistic Daisy I adored. I had just enough energy and focus in me to make that connection. "What happened, Daisy? And you are not stupid. Stop saying that about yourself."

"I can't help it." She wailed softly, a sound that from anyone else—like me—would have come across as pathetic but instead felt endearing. "He's right, I'm dumb and will never amount to anything."

Ah, no. No, no, nope, uh-uh, no freaking way. No man ever, *ever*, got to tell her she was stupid. "Emile," I growled.

She shrugged just a little, head down, tears dripping into her scotch. "He's right."

"He's a dick." I shook her a bit and she finally met my eyes. "What triggered this?"

"He wants me to go back to Luxembourg City with him," she said. "And I said no."

"And that makes you stupid." Right.

"Emile thinks I'm wasting my life in Reading." She wiped delicately at her nose. "He's right, Fee. I am wasting it. I've been coasting for so long and I just have never had the courage to go after what I really want. Not like you." She sniffed. "You're so brave and I wish I could be more like you."

"You," I said, "are perfect just as you are." And I was a horrible, horrible friend. Because this obviously wasn't a new thing for Daisy. She was too broken up about it for it to be something she hadn't been thinking about for a while now. "What do you want to do?"

She shrugged, sighed. "That's the problem. I don't know."

"Well," I said, "time to find out." She laughed a little at my finger snap and head tilt as I winked at her. "Do you want to go all the way to the other side of the pond with Mr. Douchenozzle McJerkface?"

Now she really laughed. "I do *not*," she said emphatically enough I knew she wasn't just saying that. "But I am grateful for the kick in the pants." Leave it to Daisy to see the sunny side.

"You saved my butt when I moved back here," I said. "Coming to work at Petunia's like you did. But Daisy, I know you're not happy there." She opened her mouth, a protest waiting, but I cut her off. "You're welcome every day of the week as long as you want to stay. But your happiness is far more important. And I can find someone else if you need to go uncover what it is you're looking for."

She hugged me and I hugged her back and it would have been a perfect bestie moment. Except, of course, for the slow clap and sarcastic voice that interrupted.

"How adorable," Vivian said with that kind of cold judgment that immediately got my back up. "And utterly cloying."

CHAPTER TWENTY-NINE

S HE WAS THE LAST person I wanted to see just now, in her still flawless gown and her diamonds and her perfect curls piled around that sparkling tiara that made me want to jerk it off her head and throw it as hard as I could into the still cascading water feature.

"Oh, look," Daisy said in her brightest voice, "Crew let you out of your room."

Burn. Super sick burn, at that. And delivered in the nicest possible way from the girl everyone underestimated at the slightest turn. I had to bite the inside of my cheek to keep from snorting a laugh in Vivian's face as the self-proclaimed Queen of the

New England Bakery scowled at Daisy like she was trying to sort out if she'd just been insulted or not.

"I'm looking for him," she said at last. Sniffed in our general direction and I realized Daisy had nailed it on the head so hard I had to fight off another outburst. He'd done just as my friend said, dumped Vivian in her room and left her there by herself all evening. Left me wide open for a delicious attack, too.

"We've been investigating," I said. "Mayor's orders. While she's been in the penthouse, you know. Entertaining all the visiting funders."

Vivian's face went pale, two bright, pink spots all that remained of her color on the peaks of her cheekbones. "He said we all had to stay in our rooms." And now he was in serious doodoo and I wasn't the least bit guilty over it either.

"I guess that just referred to people who weren't important," I said. "I'm sure he'll explain it later. When he has time for you."

Now, I'm not normally a vindictive person. Well, at least, not this vindictive. But Vivian woke in me the old hurts, the memories of hating my life in Reading thanks to her and my cousin Robert—now a deputy and happy to rub in he had the job I always wanted—and their horrible little posse who did their best to make me feel small. Daisy had been my only real friend and I'd abandoned her, I was now realizing, standing there in the quiet bar with the sound of water falling and Vivian's hateful stare that exact same hateful stare I remembered from ten years ago. And knew exactly how Elizabeth Adler must have felt, except she made the mistake of trying to fit in. I wasn't so smart, tried to go it alone and suffered for it.

Until I turned then with grief in my heart to meet my best friend's eyes and totally let go of the mean, spiteful woman hating me from across the room in favor of the one who had only ever had my back. So, not Elizabeth after all. Lucky me.

"Day," I whispered. "How can you ever forgive me for leaving you here?"

She shook her head and smiled, sad but kinder than I deserved. "I didn't have the courage to go," she said, "and I didn't have the heart to ask you to stay."

I really sucked as a friend, didn't I?

"Oh, please," Vivian snapped, returning my attention to her, "find somewhere else to have your sad girl moment. Where the rest of us don't have to gag on your patheticness."

"Crew's in the dining room," I said, dismissing her with those words. And ignored her when she huffed at me before stomping to the exit. Pausing one last time to throw daggered words at us.

"Tell him I'm more important than some stupid dead body," she snarled. "And that he can find me with the people who really matter." With that, she was gone, heels clicking on the tile until she crossed from the bar to the foyer and was gone. Thank god.

"And that," I said, "is why I left Reading, Vermont."

Daisy nodded. "I know."

"Just sucks," I said. "I should have made you come with me, Day."

She laughed then, tossed her head, perfect updo not moving an inch. "Silly. I would have just cried and asked you to stay home and we wouldn't have parted as we did."

"Friends." I smiled at her.

"The best of." She hugged me again. "As for Vivian. She's just jealous. She knows full well Crew isn't in to her no matter how hard she tries."

"He's here with her," I said. "Sharing a room with her."

"Says who?" Daisy's arched eyebrow was back with a vengeance. "That little yellow birdie is on her own tonight, I'll have you know. Though, she might find someone to take her home if the mayor has her way."

Vivian would love that. Marry money, divorce with no prenup and marry money again. From what I'd uncovered since arriving home, it wouldn't be the first time.

Oh, Fee. So cynical.

I really shouldn't have felt better about Crew after Daisy's little reveal, but a hardened part of my poor, battered heart warmed at the understanding he'd been a pawn in yet another of Vivian's games. I really needed to stop giving her my belief and lean toward the skeptical when it came to every word that came out of her mouth. Yes, they'd shared a selfie. So what? It was likely she made sure she was sitting with him for that reason. And the whole show at the first of the night, entering the bar like she owned it, ahead of him? Probably either a stupid coincidence or her being sneaky and setting it up so I'd see them together like that.

Naw, she wasn't that clever. Probably her good luck and my bad.

"You likely don't remember when Vivian was skinny and ugly like the rest of us," Daisy said, sipping her scotch before wrinkling her nose and pushing it away.

"Um, no," I said, "not like the rest of us. I recall you were always gorgeous."

She dimpled and batted her lashes. "Point is, behind the fake boobs and the injections and the dye job and those tinted contacts, she's not all that."

Tell me about it. Who wore contacts that blue they looked fake?

All the air left my body in a rush as I exhaled like someone just slapped me. And, in a giant moment of clarity, I almost passed out from the forced lack of oxygen. Because I suddenly knew exactly who killed Mason. Who tried to kill me. And why.

"Daisy," I hugged her again, hurrying away as I yelled back over my shoulder at her, "thank you!"

CHAPTER THIRTY

I HAD TO FIND Dad and Crew immediately. Like, this very second, before I could let go of the gigantic epiphany that washed away everything, including my weakness and how tired I'd just been. Even burning off the last of the alcohol I'd just ingested. Because holy crap on a cracker. If I was right, my weary neurons actually firing correctly at last? Yeah, this had turned into a ghost hunt of massive proportions.

Crew wasn't in the dining room, the door open, the body gone. So he'd moved James somewhere he could protect, then? And Mason's body, probably to the freezer, if he was thinking straight and done with the remains as an interrogation tool. Nothing grosser than the idea of Mason Patterson slowly composting on the stage under that hideous sheet that had been a tablecloth. The seeping smear of chocolate over the lump of his face and other foods just made my stomach churn.

As for Dad, I knew he had to be where Crew was, likely with Ethan. And when I spun to head for the front desk, panic struck me. I was out of time. They'd just have to catch up later. Because no way was I letting the murderer go free.

"Where is Paisley?" I practically assaulted Donna Walker as she emerged from the office, her face tight with the same kind of weariness that had muffled my brain enough it took a comment from Daisy to shake me out of my muzzy haze and finally connect the dots.

She shook her spiky red head, looking around. "I have no idea," she said. "She was here just a moment ago."

She must have seen me heading for Crew and guessed I'd put two and two together. Or had finally decided to cut her losses and run for the hills. But there was now zero doubt in my mind that Paisley was the murderer. The question remained, though— was this a ghost hunt? Was she Elizabeth Adler, too?

I ran for the staff quarters and stopped at the exit doors just before I could reach the keypad. Stared at the exit, thought about the missing snowmobile. And winced as my shoulder hit the door and I stumbled outside, lurching into the snow. At least this time I was in warmer clothes, but not that warm. Really, what had I been thinking? The storm raged bigger and louder than ever, and I realized far too late Petunia had followed me, chugged her little legs and her fat pug body in pursuit of me as she had all evening and I'd failed to realize it. Guilt punched me in the gut, drove me to bend in the stiff wind despite my woozy bout with dizziness. I hefted Petunia into my arms and ran the opposite way from my botched escape attempt last time, hearing Bill's voice in my head.

That door leads to the back entry to the ski lifts. The instructors use it sometimes as a short cut even though I tell them not to.

The wind died as I turned the corner, the funnel of it cleaning the path, showing me the last trace of a footprint disappearing in the falling snow and I knew I was on the right track. Darkness loomed out of the blowing storm, a door appearing ahead of me, the towering construction of the ski lift appearing like a monster in the whipping white. I found the handle with one burning hand, the cold hitting me hard, Petunia whimpering in my arms, and threw us both inside, closing the door as quietly as I could behind me. My choice of escape route the first time wasn't lost on me, the fact that had I turned right instead of left Bill wouldn't have had to rescue me at all.

Terrible instincts with directions and people? This had been an educational night.

I leaned against the closed door a moment before setting my pug down on the floor and blinking into the darkness, feet sliding on the line of snow that the storm forced under the door and my entrance—and the killer's—let in. A light ahead flickered, more emergency illumination. Obviously the generators weren't feeding this section because no one in their right mind would be out here on a night—early morning—like this one. Except the murderer of Mason Patterson trying to escape on a stolen snowmobile.

I caught sight of the puffy parka, the fluff of white fur around the collar. The same one from the office I'd noticed earlier tonight, dripping snow and melting fast. Just before Bill mentioned the loss of the machine he'd been hunting ever since.

"Clever," I called out. "But you'll die out there for real this time if you try to escape in the storm, Elizabeth."

She spun, stared me down, frozen a moment with her hands on the controls of the ski lift, the bulky box of a small, silent generator at her feet. "You've got it all wrong, Miss Fleming," Paisley said. "I'm not Elizabeth Adler."

Well, crap. "But you did murder Mason."

She leaned sideways, hand dropping to her side, rising with something long and skinny in her grasp. For the second time in two months I stared down the barrel of a gun, only this one an odd looking rifle and in hands far steadier than Peggy Munroe's had been. I'd been scared when my elderly neighbor tried to kill me. But not with the chill certainty I felt now. Peggy had been cold and calculating and horrible. This girl, whoever she really was, had cracked completely. I'd never seen such an expression utterly devoid of humanity.

And I'd wanted to hire her? Man, I really did have the worst instincts about people ever.

"I did." She shrugged like his death meant nothing to her.

"Why?" I held out both hands, Petunia shivering as she sat on my feet, my own body reacting to the cold. While we were out of the storm it was still below freezing in here and I didn't know how long I'd survive even if she didn't shoot me. I needed to call for help, my cell phone lost somewhere outside thanks to Paisley I now knew. But the curiosity in me wouldn't let me run or try to escape. Not until I understood. And, the longer I kept her talking… maybe the boys would find me.

Yeah, wishful thinking.

She hesitated at the question. "Why do you care?"

For the briefest instant I saw my survival in the flash of vulnerability in her face. So there was someone inside that hard and frozen shell of nothing she showed me. Maybe with a little urging and kindness I could find a way to stay alive and get her to stand down.

"Because he was a jerk and from what I understand probably deserved to die." My turn to shrug. "And because I want to know how he hurt you so much. I thought we'd made a connection." I swallowed the bile rising in the back of my throat as I spoke, disgusted with myself. "All night I've been thinking about offering you a job, trying to poach you from the lodge to work for me at Petunia's." My pug groaned at the sound of her name, looked up at me with those huge, trusting eyes. I couldn't let us both down. She'd saved my life when Peggy tried to kill me. I had to do the job this round and pay her back.

When I looked up again and met Paisley's gaze, she blinked, lips curving downward, her expression returning to that soft vulnerability I'd seen before. It lasted longer this time, though her hands shifted on the skeleton of a rifle as if she fought her own heart.

"You were?" She sounded so young, so fragile. "Why would you do that?"

"Because I like you," I said. "And I thought we were friends."

She looked away, snuffled, the gun's mouth lowering a little, a flap open where the muzzle ended. I'd seen a rifle like this before, but where? "I don't have any friends," she said.

My mind made a leap. "You had Elizabeth."

Paisley's head whipped around and she stared at me, jaw tightening, eyes snapping back to that cold and empty expression. And, as they did, I recognized her at last, as the lurker in the background of Mason's photos. Not Elizabeth at all in the blue hoody, the red sweater either. Or, maybe, taking turns in that position. If I looked more closely, would there be two lurkers instead of one?

"What's your real name, Paisley?" I'd almost lost her, but maybe I could bring her back.

"It doesn't matter, now," she snapped. "I never mattered, not even to Liz, not after that last birthday." She stumbled to a halt, voice cracking. "How was I supposed to know? No one told me. I made the cake just for him and it was supposed to be special. He was supposed to *like* me."

The cake. "You almost killed Mason."

She nodded. "And Elizabeth died because of it."

CHAPTER THIRTY-ONE

I TOOK A HALF step forward, Petunia grunting in protest but sliding sideways and following me as I eased toward the girl who seemed suddenly locked in the past, her head down, the gun pointing at the ground again. My dog had made zero effort to run to the girl and greet her, clinging to me as if she understood here was someone she needed to avoid at all costs. And whether Petunia stayed with me to protect me— there was precedence, after all—or for protection, I wasn't sure. Didn't care. Having her there was equal parts guilt over not making sure she was safe ages ago and gratitude not to be alone, even if it was one chubby pug on my side against crazy.

A closer examination of the rifle rang some bells as I moved closer. The lodge's logo was etched in the side, the butt a metal plate with holes in it what I needed to make the connection. Not a regular gun but a biathlon rifle. Great, Olivia's badgering to have a team here gave the murderer a weapon to steal. Not like she wouldn't have dug up a gun somewhere, I guess. And if she picked one, at least it was a small caliber. Still, a .22 would kill me with the right aim and regardless of its original intended use.

"Tell me your name," I said, as softly and kindly as I could, hoping to encourage her to talk and yet not shake free of her dazed stillness. "I really want to know."

She sniffed, a large drop of moisture falling from her chin and catching the illumination of the emergency light, turning it into a bright red spot before it hit the concrete floor. "Jenny. Jenny Markham."

"It's nice to meet you, Jenny," I said. My gaze examined the gun again quickly, unable to stop myself from thinking about the obvious threat. How many bullets did it hold? Did she have to reload between shots? I couldn't remember, desperate mind trying to make a plan. Deadly, especially for Petunia, but maybe I could take a hit somewhere unimportant if I needed to.

Wait, was I honestly considering letting her shoot me? Weaponless and without backup or anyone knowing where I was, yeah. Kind of out of other options.

"I knew you were on to me," Jenny said, voice lowering though the sadness had gone, the flat line sound returning. "The contact lens, right?"

"I didn't make the connection," I said. "Not until a few minutes ago. But I did wonder why anyone would wear brown lenses. Everyone I've met who uses color contacts picks a brighter tone."

She shrugged. "My eyes are blue," she said. "And I used to be a brunette. But you know that already."

"You were the girl in the photos." I nodded to her.

"One of them." Her lips tightened as if she wished she hadn't admitted that, then twisted into a snarl. "The one you called the lurker." The gun came up again, pointing directly at me, anger now showing on her face. I'd come close enough I could make out her pale eyes. She'd shed the fake contacts. With her hair in shadow dressed in the bulky parka she was definitely more the girl from the photos than the

Paisley I'd come to know behind the desk. "The girl no one noticed."

"Elizabeth noticed you," I said. "She was your friend."

"She wasn't." Jenny surprised me with that, wiping at her nose quickly with one hand before grasping the rifle firmly again. Damn it, too slow. But tackling a young woman with a loaded gun wasn't exactly the smartest thing to consider, especially now that I could see the magazine holding who knew how many shots. She didn't have to reload. Peggy's gun held multiple rounds, too but she had already been on the ground when I disarmed her thanks to Petunia. But despite Dad's training in handling weapons, I didn't see a way around taking a bullet at this point.

Well, damn it.

"You tried to kill me," I said, putting as much hurt in my voice as I could, matching hers.

Jenny flinched, looked away again. "You were on to me," she said. "Or you would have been. I just needed you out of the way." She seemed confused, a bit disoriented by the change of topic.

"Did you know I'd die out there, Jenny?" This girl was nuts.

She shook her head, met my gaze again, hers twisted in guilt. "Did I? I don't know. Yes, maybe. Yes." She was trembling now, shaking all over, the gun vibrating in her hands. And while her unsteadiness was a good thing, her finger on the trigger wasn't the optimal position for Petunia and I staying alive and unharmed. Jenny stilled suddenly, like a switch flipping inside her brain and I knew then I was right. She'd lost her mind and there wasn't anything I could do to talk her down.

Petunia and I were so screwed.

"This wasn't supposed to happen." The faint wail in her voice made my ears ache. I shivered steadily now, hugging myself, knowing the cold was going to make escape impossible. I couldn't go out into the storm in this condition, not and carry Petunia and make it back to the lodge. Though, if I could get around Jenny, I might be able to reach the staff door under the lift or even the corridor to the lobby.

I just had to get past the crazy girl with the rifle.

"The storm," I said, brain slowing as the cold took its toll but still with me enough to make that connection. "You didn't plan on the weather."

"Everything was perfect," she snarled, stomping one booted foot. "And then the damned storm came out of nowhere. But it was too late, I had my perfect plan in motion and no one suspected me. No one." She glared then. "Except you."

I had a horrible feeling about the rest of her story, knew encouraging her to talk was the only thing keeping me alive. And though I figured it was a 50/50 between disabling her already broken mind and feeding her anger enough to trigger my death, I prodded her anyway.

"Elizabeth," I said. "Jenny, do you know what happened to her?" I hesitated when she froze and stared at me like she didn't see me. It was a fight to keep my teeth from chattering when I spoke again. "Why did you kill Mason? Because he killed her?"

"No," she whispered, barely audible over the whistling wind outside and my own shivering. "Because he picked her over me."

I swallowed and stayed quiet, waiting for her to finish. She couldn't help herself now, it was clear on her face, how it twisted, her gaze locked into the distant past as she relived what happened in her mind. While I again began to ease sideways toward her.

"She was my best friend. Liz and me, from the moment we met at college. I never had a best friend." Jenny smiled faintly, one hand releasing the rifle to touch the air in front of her like she saw Elizabeth before her. I had to force myself to keep moving slowly, still sliding around her left side, away from the hand supporting the gun and toward the generator. There was a metal hose draped over it, the open end stuffed into the workings of the machine. One glance at the wall gave me the source of that hose, a shutoff valve and an explosive sign pretty clear in their meaning. What was she planning? It couldn't be good. "We had so much in common and we both loved him. Both of us. Equally. And that was okay." She nodded, her smile tight now, then collapsing as tears trickled down her face. "Until I made him that cake." She choked on a sob. "And he blamed Elizabeth. I never told her. I couldn't." Her head shake made me freeze a moment, fearful she'd jerk herself out of her reverie but she was lost in the past and I was close, so close. "I thought we'd be best friends forever. I comforted her, I was there for her when he was so cruel. My fault." She lowered her head. "My fault he thought she tried to kill him."

I stopped my advance, Petunia huffing softly as she leaned into me for warmth or support or whatever motivated her doggy brain. Damn it, just two more steps and I could get my hands on the rifle. Two more.

Jenny looked up, snapped back to reality. And those few feet were suddenly far too close for comfort.

"If that bitch Ava hadn't saved Mason, none of this would have happened." Jenny shrugged. "I wish I'd had time to kill her, too, but she'll just have to suffer with everyone else."

Wait, what? "What are you talking about?"

"The generators," she said. "I rigged them with the gas lines." She gestured at her feet, the hose I'd noticed. "This place is state of the art." She sounded proud of that. "Solar panels, geothermal heating systems. But most of it isn't up and running yet so they're using natural gas." She giggled then, a little girl in a broken young woman's mind. "Did you know gas and electricity make for an impressive combination? Once I turn this one on and get things pumping, the others should blow in minutes."

Wait, what? "What others?" Stupid and slow, Fee.

"The main genset of course," Jenny said. "The whole thing's rigged to go up in a glorious fashion. I'll be up the mountain by then. I'm sure it will be a beautiful show." She smiled then, wide and so creepy

I flinched. "Daddy was a mechanic and his little girl learned lots." Her fingers tightened on the rifle stock. "Including how to shoot to kill."

CHAPTER THIRTY-TWO

"WAIT, PLEASE." I HELD up both hands, trembling from the cold and fear. "The rest of the story, Jenny. What happened to Elizabeth? What happened to your best friend?"

I needed her to fall back into that state of distance, because it wasn't just me at risk anymore. Panic spiked inside me, my heart pounding. While the generator explosion might not reach inside the main lodge, all the staff was confined to their section. And from what Bill showed me, the generators sat literally on the other side of their quarters. It was highly likely at least some of them would die. And if a fire broke out, the whole lodge could be affected. I had to disarm her. Now.

But Jenny wasn't falling for my tactics again, whether due to her renewed focus or my loss of compassion thanks to my terror. Instead, she jerked the gun in my direction and smiled with a cruel twist to her mouth. "We were supposed to be friends forever. She promised. And that we'd always love him equally. But she changed that. She lied."

"Mason asked her to go skiing." I let that hang in the frosty air.

Jenny flinched. "She invited me to Aspen." She sounded like that had been a dream, something she'd never get to do otherwise. "I thought we were going to spend the whole week together. But then he broke our code. He divided the sisterhood." Jenny's jaw jumped, blue eyes snapping fury. "And she let him, the traitor. She tossed me to the side and destroyed our trust and went skiing with him that day instead of doing what she swore she'd do."

"She betrayed you and broke your heart." I nodded, hugging myself again to try to conserve some heat. While tensing and preparing for the worst. Because as soon as I gathered the courage, I was going to leap at her and likely get shot and there was nothing else I could do about it. There was zero doubt in my mind, gazing into her hard and pitiless eyes, that she was going to shoot me regardless. I might as well go out trying to be a hero.

"I followed them up the mountain," she said. "Watched him leave her there. They all did. They abandoned her at the top of that black diamond. She cried, did you know that? She just stood there and cried and I watched her from the woods and I hated her for crying over them."

"What happened, Jenny?" I didn't mean to sound so compassionate but maybe it was the cold, the weakness, the weariness. But I suddenly saw her there, watching her only friend weep over people who didn't give a crap about her, while the one person who did care turned from twisted, damaged love to utter hate.

Whatever the cause of my authentic empathy, it reached her, if only for a moment. Jenny stilled, lips working before she spoke. "I was on snowshoes," she said. "I couldn't ski. But it didn't matter. Made it easier to sneak up behind her while she cried. The run was supposed to be closed so there was no one around. So quiet. And snowing just a little. Peaceful except for her blubbering." Jenny exhaled deeply like the story was just too heavy for her to carry anymore. "I hit her over the head with a rock. And dragged her into the woods before rolling her over a cliff where no one would ever find her." Jenny paused, tilted her head, face stilling from that hard fury to utter calm. "She bounced on the bottom, twice. But she never made a sound."

I couldn't speak, not for a long time. Didn't matter. Jenny went on without me.

"I tried, after that, you know." She stared down at her hands on the rifle, a faint smile on her lips. "I totally remade myself." That tiny expression turned to a beaming smile. "Lost weight, changed my clothes, tried to fit in. Because that was what he wanted. Wasn't it what he wanted?"

I nodded, still tongue tied by her admission of her casual and horrific murder of Elizabeth Adler.

"None of it mattered," Jenny said, crying again though her face twisted in rage. "Not even a little. Because he was all about Ava from then on. Ava, Ava, Ava." Her knuckles whitened on the rifle, her teeth audibly grinding while my own clattered in my head.

"But you didn't kill her," I said.

"I didn't," she said. "Not directly. Because she doesn't matter, not anymore. She didn't make me kill my best friend." Blue eyes snapped with insanity. "Mason did. That worthless trash got between us. It was his fault and he paid for it." She seemed flustered then, hesitant. "And now I have nothing."

"You have so much, Jenny," I said. "Please, don't do this. Just turn yourself in. I know they'll understand. They'll see what you went through, I'm sure of it."

Her jaw jutted at me, grief flashing to blank emptiness. "You're just afraid because I'm going to shoot you."

Petunia muttered something, grumbling as she shivered against me. I glanced down at her and felt for the third time in less than a year that I was going to die. And no Moose barreling out of the snow to save me, no Petunia to take Peggy out at the knees. Just the cold and the rifle and the crazy girl with zero crap to give.

"The peanut oil," I gasped, desperate to keep her talking if only to stay alive a few more minutes. "You stole it from the kitchen?"

She seemed bored at last, rolling her eyes. "Easy," she said. "Why Chef had it anyway, knowing Mason was allergic. Whatever. I had some with me regardless. But it gave me a great opportunity to deflect suspicion."

"Onto Ethan," I said.

"He's just as pathetic as Elizabeth was," Jenny snapped. "Fawning over that Ava even though she didn't love him. I saw it, I saw everything. How they all treated each other, how Mason manipulated them against one another. I'm surprised Noah didn't find a way to betray Ethan before now. He owed his soul to Mason, was always at Ava to leave his brother for his master. Sickening, all of them."

"You hid the oil in the men's washroom on purpose," I said. "Placed the out of order sign."

"I had him touch it earlier," she said. "Asked him to hold it. He had no idea what it was."

"So his finger prints are on it." I nodded, sighed. "You really would have gotten away with it."

Jenny grinned her crazy ass grin. "I still will," she said. "Because the only person who knows the truth is about to eat a bullet."

"You erased the security footage," I said, a bit hasty, fear driving words out of my mouth. "You know, you're a great actor, Jenny. Oscar worthy performance in there. All of it. Truly masterful."

She curtsied a little, even giggled. Did nothing to make me feel better about my odds.

"I had you fooled, but I knew better. Those sheriffs were off on the wrong ideas from the start. But I saw the smart in you, Fiona. I figured you'd be onto me eventually. I really hoped I wouldn't have to do this. That you'd die in the snow. I don't want to have to shoot you."

"You were at the desk when the cake was served," I said.

"Oh, please," she laughed. "Everyone was in the dining room, Donna with Chef and with Nancy gone home because of her stupid baby I had the run of the place. There's a back entry to the kitchen. I just found the slice with the candle on the table and used the oil on it. Two seconds flat."

"And the vial under Simone's chair?" I was at the end of my questions. This was it. I was going to die shortly after she answered. Maybe we both knew it because the already tense atmosphere tightened further and Jenny's aim stilled to a pinpoint.

"Placed there long before dinner was served," Jenny said. "Thanks for the chance to get all of that off my chest. It's been cathartic." There was nothing to say to that. "Goodbye, Miss Fleming."

CHAPTER THIRTY-THREE

I TENSED TO LEAP, knowing this was the end, terrified for Petunia, for the lodge, for myself. Drew a breath in slow motion while everything seemed to still and fall silent, my heartbeat thudding from one da-dum to the next before stopping as time stood as frozen as the mountain.

Petunia's bark broke the instant, shattered Jenny's focus, my terror. I fell to my knees and hugged her, the gun swinging toward her, the crazy girl's expression twisting and I knew then my pug would go first if I didn't act.

Even as the door across from her opened and four people walked in so casually from the staff quarters, arguing above the storm's echoing wind, they clearly had no idea what they'd just interrupted.

I don't know what prompted them to come, didn't care at the moment. I was just ridiculously happy to see them and then horrified they were now at risk, too. Had I still been on my feet I would have risked throwing myself at Jenny, but I'd lost my position, hugging the pug I'd come to love and staring up at the crazy girl while she backed away from me, her weapon now leveled at Simone, Ava, Noah and Ethan who froze as they finally realized they were in danger.

"What the hell?" Ethan raised both hands to Jenny while Noah hid behind his brother, Ava looking back and forth between her and me like she couldn't comprehend what she was seeing, Simone huddling next to her. "Put the gun down, miss."

"Miss." Jenny barked that word in a laugh that sounded painful. "You see?" She swung the gun toward me again before lashing it back at the four friends. "He doesn't even know my name."

"Paisley, right?" Ava's voice had that soft and soothing tone one used on a frightened animal. At least she was in control of herself. "You work the front desk."

"This is Jenny Markham," I said. "You go to school with her. She was Elizabeth's best friend." I stressed every syllable, aiming my attention at Ava and Simone. Two sets of eyes widened as they nodded to me.

"Right, Jenny. I remember now." Ava forced casualness, in her tone, in the way she tucked her hands into her trendy snow jacket.

"Yes, of course. Nice to see you again." Simone tilted her head at me, fear as clear as her confusion while my sad heart realized neither of them did know who Jenny was. So the crazy girl had that much right.

Ethan wasn't getting the hint. "What's going on? I don't understand."

"This is perfect." Jenny laughed again. "I had hoped at least the generator accident would hurt you, maybe kill you. I couldn't risk making sure. But now?" She pointed the weapon at Ethan. "I can take all of you out and the explosion will hide everything."

"She's rigged the generators," I said in a low voice, forcing myself to my feet, my pug in my arms. Because I refused to let Jenny shoot her. "She killed Mason and Elizabeth."

Not that I had to state the obvious or anything.

"Jenny, you don't have to do this." Poor Ava had no idea I'd tried that line already.

"No, I guess not," she said suddenly, rifle tip dropping. "In fact, I only need you, don't I?" Jenny gestured for Ava to come closer. "You're coming with me or I'm killing everyone here and making you watch."

"Ava." Ethan grabbed for her but she was already moving, hands out of her pockets and held out in surrender while the other three gathered together and let her sacrifice herself for them. My entire being cracked in that instant and I understood Jenny's hate with the kind of piercing disappointment that I'd only felt once before—when Ryan cheated and I left him.

"You can't go far," I said. "Not in this storm." Petunia held very still in my arms as I straightened, shivers fading, last remaining dose of adrenaline forcing my shoulders back and my resolve to stiffen like my cold limbs.

"Watch me." She spared one second to lean down and press the button on the generator beside her, then straightened and pulled the lever for the lift. The same one she'd been reaching for when I interrupted her first. With a belching roar from the generator, power bloomed around us, the giant cogs and chains of the lift coming to life, the garage door folding upward, exposing us to the storm. The wind whipped past the opening, adding to the thrum of sound, pure white on the other side, stirring little tornadoes of snow but at the wrong angle, thankfully, to blast us with its full power. The lift itself hummed and groaned slowly up to speed, the first bench seat sliding gracefully upward and out into the storm. "I'll leave her for you at the top of the mountain," Jenny called out over the grumble of the generator and the howl of winter. "Somewhere."

"The snowmobile," I yelled. "You drove it up there earlier." The temperature in here had already been cold but now it was dropping fast. I had to find a way to end this. Especially now that the natural gas lines were working and, if she was telling the truth, pumping fuel into the intakes of not only her small generator but the genset of the entire lodge. So little time to stop the chain reaction of devastation she'd set in motion.

"And skied down," she shouted back. "I've learned, since last winter." She grabbed for Ava, nabbed the sleeve of her jacket, tugged her close with the rifle steady in her other hand. Her right hand.

Smart despite her insanity. "Get on." She shoved Ava toward the lift, following her with her back to the girl.

I caught Ava's attempt to subdue Jenny just as she made it, the shift in her stance, the way her face tightened. And leaped, not for the girl with the gun, but the generator only a few feet away. Petunia yipped in pain as I landed against the machine with her squashed against me and kicked the hose, gas hissing as it skipped across the concrete. I didn't have time to worry about possible sparks and the fact I might have just killed us all in my haste, fist coming down on the big red button on the generator's lid. It died instantly, cutting off the power and the noise in the same instant Ava lashed out at Jenny's gun hand, sending the rifle spinning. It landed and skidded toward the big doors, now gaping open, and the two girls leaped for it together.

"Get her!" My shout at the three huddled friends did nothing, though it turned out we didn't need them. Not when a giant, black shadow, growling loud enough to be heard despite the storm, leaped from the snow and landed on Jenny.

Moose, his massive body pinning her to the ground, howled his victory while an equally large form lurched from the snow and retrieved the rifle.

"I think you dropped this," Bill said to the weeping Jenny trapped under his grinning dog.

CHAPTER THIRTY-FOUR

I STOOD, SHIVERING DESPITE my warm jacket, hat and mitts, heavy winter boots to my knees, on the front step of the lodge and inhaled the crisp, winter air while the line of guests exited the foyer and headed for the parking lot. The plows rumbled by, clearing another strip of snow from the main road, pushing back the last of the heavy whiteness and letting us leave at last.

Daylight never felt so good and despite the crispness of the air the sun warmed my cheeks enough in the shelter of the building, the quiet calm a huge change from the storm, I was loathe to go back inside. I was packed and ready, but wanted to wait until everything was finished before I took my leave.

Two state troopers exited the building with Jenny between them, Crew trailing after them, talking in a low voice. He descended the main stairs to their car, finishing his conversation while one of them helped the girl into the back of the car and slammed the door. I swallowed hard, heart pounding, and admitted this was the reason I lingered. For proof that she was safely in custody, for an instant of connection as her eyes lifted and met mine. She smiled, cracked and broken, before lowering her head and not looking up again.

Crew joined me as they drove away, hands in his pockets, steam rising from his lips while he exhaled heavily. "The state boys will have a fight on their hands once the FBI comes sniffing around," he said. "Elizabeth's murder in Colorado makes it a case they'll both fight over."

I shrugged, sad and wanting to be warm again, turning toward the foyer and my bags waiting behind the desk. "Let them. I'm just as happy to wash my hands of anything to do with this whole mess."

Crew held the door for me with a lip twist of agreement. "For once, I'm with you, Fee."

My boots thudded on the carpet when I crossed to the desk, Mom waiting there with Petunia between them. But my mission to leave wasn't quite over, not when I almost stumbled into James Adler and Lucas Day. The pair hesitated as they paused before me and I realized Crew had followed me, was now standing next to me while the tall, lean Adler spoke.

"I wanted to thank both of you," he said, "for finding Elizabeth's murderer. She deserved justice."

I squeezed his hand and nodded. "I'm so sorry," I said. "But at least now you'll be able to find her body." Jenny had given up enough details search and rescue teams in Aspen were already looking.

"Lucas and I have been friends a long time," James said, smiling to the other man with tears in his eyes. "I've missed that friendship since I lost my daughter. But you gave that back to me, too."

"To both of us." Lucas clasped his partner's hand. "That matters to me more than any real estate deal, James."

"What does that mean?" I really needed sleep because I was blurting random questions at people who seemed to have found some happy I didn't need to be disturbing.

But James sighed like he'd been pondering that question already. "It means there's a very good chance I'll be exiting this project, and probably declaring bankruptcy, if the Pattersons have anything to say about it." He shrugged. "They hold the 51% share and though Lucas and I are reconciled, I'm still out of luck."

"Maybe not." I hadn't expected Aundrea to appear and join the conversation bundled in a trendy and clearly expensive white snow suit that screamed big city designer. "In fact, if the two of you are up for it, this Patterson would like to discuss an agreement." She winked at me, Pamela holding Cookie in her puffy ski-jacketed arms next to her partner grinning like she knew something no one else did.

"I don't understand," Lucas said, a faint hope in his voice.

"Only that the Patterson family shares the 51% as a whole," Aundrea said, hooking one arm through James's elbow and the other through Lucas's. "And that my son and I, as Pattersons, would like to tip the scales in your favor. If that's acceptable to you."

I grinned when she led them away, heart lighter than it had been in a while. No, wait. I think that was lightheadedness from needing to fall down and sleep this whole crap show off.

Crew shook his head, rubbing at his temples. "This town," he whispered, "will be the death of me."

I jabbed him in the ribs with one elbow and laughed with a snort at the end, knowing I sounded vaguely like a protesting donkey and not really caring. "Careful what you wish for."

Crew grunted to me before striding off like it was the only response he had left.

As I turned to head for Mom and my dog again, arms wrapped around me, pulling me tight and almost choked me with enthusiasm. I hugged Simone back, looking up at her when she finally released me, her dark eyes brimming with tears and dark cheeks already wet.

"I'm so sorry, Fee," she whispered. "I just stood there and watched and couldn't move, couldn't do anything. I was so scared." She sniffled, hands shaking as they grasped mine. "Jazz was right. You're so much braver than anyone else I know."

I embraced her again and sighed out the moment of disappointment I'd felt, knowing it wasn't real, induced by terror and Jenny and exhaustion. "Just do me a favor," I said. "No more jerks."

She laughed, pulled away, sniffling and brightening at the same time. "I swear to you, I'm done. Dating them and being one. Nice guys and kind Simone from now on. And not even any kind of love life for a while." She hugged herself, her puffy navy coat squishing around her before she dropped her arms and smiled at me in that way that made me miss her sister like crazy. "I think I might look at law school." She winked. "If Jazz won't mind a lawyer in the family."

I laughed. "You know how your social worker sister feels about lawyers. Good luck with that."

She left me there, dragging her rollie to the door and exiting out into the sunshine while I shook my head and wished her the best. Turned at last and headed for my mother, my pug, and home.

CHAPTER THIRTY-FIVE

AS I FOCUSED ON my goal, I caught movement from the dining room doors and glanced that way in time to see Dad and Malcolm Murray emerging from the quiet of the hall. For a moment they paused, Malcolm's hand on Dad's arm and my father actually waiting, head down, listening as The Orange's Irish owner whispered something to him. Dad shook his head and walked away at last, leaving Malcolm to stare after him with a sad look on his face. I swerved without thinking, crossing to join him and when he spotted me that sorrow turned to a flash of a smile in a heartbeat.

"A busy night, Fiona," he said. "And I hear you're to thank for catching the killer."

I shrugged at that, not caring about his praise at the moment. "What were you and Dad talking about just now?" Maybe it was being overtired or just tired of secrets but I know I was a bit abrupt. Okay, more than a bit. Malcolm didn't seem to mind, though his sorrow returned around the edges of the smile that didn't fade while he spoke.

"Nothing to do with *this* murder, lass," he said, and walked away.

I stared after him, the obvious question in my mind from the way he chose to phrase his exit statement, whether consciously or not. And I highly doubted a man like Malcolm ever spoke a word without thinking.

So, to take things too far—or not far enough. If not *this* murder, then which one? What was my father hiding?

Daisy had joined Mom and my quiet dad by the time I reached them, hugging my pug against her long, wool coat, cradling the dog like a toddler against her faux fur collar while Petunia leaned into her ear scratch with a groan of utter delight. Despite her bout in the cold the pug came through without any permanent damage I could see and, to my surprise, neither had I. She'd take a trip to the vet shortly just to be sure, but a doctor visit for me wasn't necessary. How I avoided frostbite I'd never know but would always be grateful.

Must have been the shots of scotch with Daisy that sustained me. Sure, I'd go with that.

I was about to take Petunia from her when my friend's eye line shifted from me to someone behind me. I turned and watched with my mouth hanging open as her former, if temporary, beau Emile strode past in a heavy fur coat of some kind of dead animal that could have used their pelt more than him as far as I was concerned. With Vivian on his arm.

"Please, Emile, wait!" So out of character to see Olivia running after anyone, let alone in a public place. She was not looking herself at all this morning, flustered and mussed, her pale cream dress from last night once elegant and perfect now wrinkled and stained, the hem showing wear.

Emile paused, Vivian with him, as the potential investor we didn't need, thank you, scowled down at the mayor. "I think I've had about enough of your hospitality," he said. "If murder and sabotage are common place in your little hamlet, I will be happy to see the back side of it. Good day, Olivia." As he spun away, the arrogant jerk, Vivian caught my gaze, Daisy's. She shot us both a vicious grin, popping an expensive pair of sunglasses down over her eyes as they runway strutted out into the sunlight, Crew scowling from his position across the foyer. Was he seriously jealous of that little show she orchestrated to make him feel crappy about himself? Well, then Vivian's plan worked, because I had zero doubt that had been her goal all along.

Olivia held very still before physically shaking off the rejection and smiling at everyone who would meet her eyes—not many people. She turned like this was just another event and a ho hum kind of day to march back toward the elevator while Mom watched her go with narrowed eyes and a speculative look on her face.

I focused on Daisy to say I was sorry about Emile only to catch her grinning.

"He's her kind of nice," she said, a long mile of meaning in that simple phrase. I couldn't help the snort that escaped. "And she's welcome to his judgmental ass."

I grinned and hugged Petunia when Daisy finally gave her up. "I meant what I said in the bar earlier. It's time. You need to find your own path, miss."

She nodded, sighed. Then her usual happy-go-lucky expression returned and she giggled before hugging Dad, Mom and then me and Petunia as a package before stepping back with a gusty sigh, arms spread, twirling in a circle like she was the queen of the world, cream wool coat flaring out around her. She'd never been so beautiful as she was in that moment.

"See you at work," she said with a wink and left with her bag over her shoulder, my incredible friend succeeding where Olivia failed, drawing every eye in the lobby whether she knew it or not.

Mom sighed. "Oh, for that kind of charisma," she said. "I'd rule the world."

Dad flinched like she'd struck him while I arched both eyebrows at her, beaming. "Or, at least, Reading," I said. "Madam Mayor?"

Mom's eyes twinkled while Dad groaned. "None of that, John Fleming," she said, expression flipping to irritation, her inner steel showing as it did so rarely. "I tolerated too many years as the sheriff's wife for you to make a peep of protest about my plans."

"Yes, dear," Dad said, gathering their bags. "Anything you say, dear. After you, dear." Mom strode off with the same kind of strut Daisy came by naturally like she was testing it out but I held Dad back a moment with a frown tightening the line between my eyes.

"Do we need to talk about Malcolm?" I waited while his face crumbled a little before he closed himself off to me. Big shocker there. But not anger, no. Sadness. What the hell was going on between those two? Or, better question, what *had* gone on?

"Love you, kid," he said, kissing my forehead before striding off after Mom with their bags in tow. Silence and secrets a la John Fleming. Okay then. We'd just see about that.

Petunia protested her confinement in my arms with a whine and a wriggle. I set her down at my feet, retrieving her harness from the top of my bag and snapping her in, retractable leash firmly secured. When I straightened up I was no longer alone, meeping a soft protest for the invasion before Ava hugged me out of nowhere, Ethan standing slightly apart, his face sad.

"Thank you," she said, bubbling over with some kind of eagerness that was infectious because I was smiling again in response to it despite my previous train of thought.

"Thank *you*," I said, squeezing her hand. "You saved our lives." I let her go. "What were you four doing out there, anyway? Talk about perfect timing."

She glanced over her shoulder at her boyfriend, looking slightly ashamed of herself. "We decided we needed to get Ethan to confess and then we were going to help him escape."

He gaped at her. "You what?"

Ava ignored his hurt reaction, returning her attention to me. "I couldn't have pulled off this happy ending without you." She was so much like me, I now realized, I worried about her and the mooning young man behind her. But when she stepped back and twined her fingers in his, Ethan's expression softened and I figured they'd earned the right to sort out if they'd be okay or not.

"We're off to Colorado," Ava said, bright with cheer. "Ethan was right. We need to move on and the jobs he set up are still waiting for us."

"Helps the national snowboarding team is there for the next three weeks," Ethan said, sadness returning, though I doubted Ava spotted it.

She squealed softly and bounced on her toes. "It's perfect." The smile she shared with him was real enough. "We're just going to see how things go from here."

"And Noah?" I didn't see him anywhere.

"Staying," Ethan said. "Figures he's the big fish in the small pond until Adler and Day figure out he's a hack and replace him." He shrugged like that was old news about his brother. "I'm sure he'll come crawling to Aspen in the next month or so and ask us to take him in."

From the firm denial on Ava's face, Noah would be in for a rough ride or Ethan would be out on his ass with his freeloader brother. Either way, I had no doubt that particular young lady was in no danger of being held back from what she wanted. And wished her the best of luck.

They left me then and I felt like I needed to get out of there or I'd be in an endless cycle of saying goodbye without the real energy to do more farewells justice. Though, as Petunia and I exited onto the front step, I spotted the final person I really wanted to talk to before we left.

Bill waved and joined us, Moose and Petunia meeting happy noses. The pair had made fast friends after Moose stopped Jenny and I found the pairing of fat fawn pug and shaggy bear of a Newfoundland hilarious.

"I wanted to make sure you were okay," I said. "And offer you a job if you need one."

Bill's look of surprise warmed my heart and made me sad at the same time.

"Thank you, Fiona," he said, "but Mr. Day and Mr. Adler want me to stay on. Said my loyalty to the lodge in the face of danger earned me a place here for as long as I want it." Thank goodness for that. He'd gone running the second I filled him in and though I knew the threat had been neutralized at the source, I had been too busy to follow up until now. "Clever, that trick of hers, feeding them natural gas." He shrugged, almost looked impressed. "If she'd been able to keep the small generator running on her way out the whole genset would have likely caught fire and blown like you said she'd planned them to." Bill sighed. "If she wasn't crazy, I'd have asked her to work for me."

As kind of nuts as that sounded, I totally understood.

"Listen, if you change your mind and go looking for contracts, you get in touch," I said. "Petunia's could use your expertise. And I know there's other people in Reading who could use a hand."

He blushed, actually smiling so bright I grinned back.

"I'd be happy to help," he said. "You just say the word."

For now, that was good enough for me. I looked down at Petunia who squatted her fat butt on the toes of my boots and stared up at me with that expression I loved so much.

"Ready to go home, your highness?" I was so ready.

She smacked her lips and farted. For some reason, I found her response incredibly hilarious and, waving goodbye to Bill and Moose, laughed all the way to my car.

CHAPTER THIRTY-SIX

I HAD TO KEEP exhaling and inhaling on purpose in order to force calm into my body, catching the bob of my foot at the end of my crossed legs before I could kick the desk in front of me one more time. My fingers, wound together tight enough I felt the impression of the key they held embedding itself permanently into my flesh, refused to unlock or let it go while I waited, heart pounding, for Tom Brackshaw to return.

With the safety deposit box my grandmother left for me.

It was hard to wait this long, to control my excitement now that Jenny was in custody for Mason's murder and our little town returning to normal after the stir the young Patterson's death had caused. Crew had been thoughtful enough to let Dad know about Mason's autopsy, to fill in the last detail that bothered me. Three minutes was a long time to struggle for air, to die. Even with the excitement of the balloons falling, surely someone besides Simone would have noticed his desperate flailing. Surely I would have. But, as it turned out, the kid didn't stand a chance. According to the coroner, the allergy attack triggered a weakness in Mason Patterson's heart. Impossible to diagnose if unsuspected, he'd suffered from a flaw in one of his arteries. It ruptured when he'd struggled for breath and killed him almost instantly. Turned out, even if he'd survived Jenny's attack, it was likely he'd have dropped dead in the next six months.

A tidbit to soothe my anxious mind as I contained my excitement for my visit to the bank. I'd forced myself to wait two whole days while plows and trucks cleaned the streets of Reading of the masses of snow that trapped residents and kept businesses closed. Two days entertaining my guests and helping Mary and Betty feed the hungry, bored visitors, two days of Petunia looking longingly into the snowy streets while power and typical small town life was restored.

I hadn't made an appointment, hoping I didn't need one. Showed up at the front desk of Reading Savings Bank with the key and little else but hope and the lingering excitement I'd been nurturing since pulling the key out of the box of letters once more and hooking it on my car ring so I wouldn't forget it this time. No chance of that. Tom's reminder in the bar that fateful night of Mason's death woke the curiosity in me all over again. To the point I could barely sleep from the wonder of what might be waiting for me.

How had I forgotten the key and its hidden treasure all these months? Some detective.

Thankfully, Tom spotted me when I arrived, caught me stammering to the receptionist what I was here to do and greeted me with that same robust jovial good nature that actually put me less at ease and not more.

He guided me quickly into his office and left me there in a flurry of his own excitement. "I'll bring it here so you don't have to go downstairs," he said. "I'll be right back!" Meanwhile, the clock over the portrait behind his chair softly tick-tick-ticked away time while he went to the vault. I should have just went with him. How could he abandon me to my anxiety and excitement like this?

No, not true anxiety. Much more on the holy crap I'm finally going to find out what this mystery was about side. And it served me right, having to wait this little time for the truth to come to me. I'd put it off for so long, somehow shunting the secret into the back of my memory in favor of the day-to-day. No longer. I was going to uncover the truth Grandmother Iris felt it so important to keep safe.

Then again, for all I knew it was a silly nothing that Grandmother Iris was laughing over up in Heaven or wherever she ended up, likely cackling while she set it up before she had her stroke. But it seemed far more possible there was a very cool light at the end of this tunnel. Especially since she'd spilled—either mistakenly or on purpose—to the dearly departed Pete Wilkins a treasure was buried in her garden.

Mind you, that came across a bit pornographic and slightly on the ewie side when I thought about it that way, reminding my poor aching brain of the brief image I'd conjured of me and Pete on a date. Yuck. But since there literally was a box buried in the ground, I could distract myself from the shudder my instincts generated and return to the bubbling anticipation that bobbed my knee, thudding my toe against the desk and locking my fingers around the key in my grasp.

Tom's door opened suddenly, without warning, a slight meep of surprise escaping me before I laughed at the hilarity of my reaction. He bustled inside, smiling that cherub beaming joy at me I remembered from being a little girl. Tom gently and almost reverently set a long, slim metal box on the desk in front of me and folded his hands over the round of his belly, grinning like this was the most fun he'd ever had.

Me too, though I doubted he could tell from my frozen state. "Thank you," I said, unable to move, barely able to fumble out those two words. What was wrong with me, really?

Tom's smile faded a bit and he cleared his throat. "I'll leave you alone then," he said.

I waved him back, freed from my moment of weirdness, shaking my head, laughing at last as the tension eased out of me. "You can stay if you want," I said. "I'm sure you're dying to know what's in here."

"It's your business," he said with great grace and aplomb. "And my pleasure." With that, he exited the room and closed the door, smiling again.

Okay then. The key fell into my lap as I forced my hands open at last, fingers cramped, the line of the key a ridged mark in my index finger. I stared down at the little strip of metal on the black plastic tag and caught a giggle before lifting the key and sliding it into the lock. It turned smoothly, the top gliding up and back and I peeked inside, stomach quivering in anticipation.

A small, elaborately carved—dare I say it, yet another—box sat inside the first, edges of painted gold and crimson reminding me of something I couldn't put my finger on. I reached inside, pulling out the rectangle on small wooden legs and then had an ah-ha moment as my fingers encountered the metal protrusion at the back.

Boxes and keys. What was Grandmother Iris trying to tell me? Well, the original one had a lock on it, but still. I made the connection as I turned the thin, metal key in the center back of the wooden box with its inlay of old red velvet and lifted the lid.

Three notes pinged at me, and three only before the sound of grinding wound them down to nothing and the music box I remembered loving as a child—one I knew the tune to and could hum if I really tried—died as the mechanism inside seized and fell silent.

For a brief moment I fought tears, the overwhelming need to sob over the little music box, the tiny ballerina still and quiet on her pedestal in the center of the opening. I gulped down the urge to cry as my throat burned and one of the loveliest memories of my childhood flared to ash and blew away.

With shaking fingers I closed the lid on the frozen dancer, and as I did my grief died. Grandmother Iris cherished this box for some reason. And I'd left it here to gather dust, done nothing to retrieve it. For all I knew, it was my fault the thing was now broken. She'd wanted me to have this music box, something I coveted from childhood and now longed for with the kind of ache that came from a lifetime of failure and self-doubt.

I stood, my grandmother's gift cradled in my hands, purse draped over my arm, jaw aching as I turned to the door. I'd find a way to fix it, to restore the precious memory she left me. And this time I wouldn't forget.

The Reading Reader Gazette

VOLUME 1 ISSUE 1   FEB 16TH. 2018   WWW.RRGAZETTE.COM

News Briefs

1. **Skiing Lessons now available:** White Valley Lodge Ski School remains open and space is available for students. Join head instructor Noah Perry for fun, interactive instruction based on your skill level and aptitude. All levels welcome, special rates for Reading residents. Snowboard lessons on request or by emailing school@wvlodge.com.

2. **Now Hiring:** White Valley Ski Lodge is now hiring for its front desk. Position to be filled immediately, experience an asset but training available. Reading residents preferred. Applicants must be bondable and twenty-one or older. Apply to the front desk and ask for Donna or submit your CV online at hiring@wvlodge.com

3. **Equestrian Center Opening Soon** Reading town council is pleased to announce the pending April 1st opening of the world class Marie Patterson Olympic Equestrian Center. With much thanks to Jared Wilkins of Wilkins Construction Inc. for timely action construction, the center will be taking applications for boarding shortly.

4. **PLEASE NOTE:** Parking rules have changed for downtown Reading during winter months. Town council would like to remind residents any cars left on the street overnight will be towed at the owner's expense. No exceptions will be permitted.

Winner of this week's Fire Hall 50/50 draw: Silvia Harris. Congratulations, Silvia!

Please send any pending community notices to: pamela@rrgazette.com before 4PM.

Valentine's Day Murder Solved

At White Valley Lodge!

Jennifer Markham of New York City, New York confessed to murdering both Elizabeth Adler, formerly of Reading and daughter of developer James Adler as well as the Valentine's Day slaying of Mason Patterson.

Death by Chocolate at newly opened White Valley Ski Lodge

By Pamela Shard

Murder was served for dessert at White Valley Lodge on Valentine's Night. the passing of Mason Erin Patterson, 21, of Reading, Vermont doled out with a dose of peanut oil dabbed onto his chocolate birthday cake. Confessed murderer Jennifer Markham, self-proclaimed college friend of Mr. Patterson, is undergoing psychiatric evaluation pending her arraignment for not only the death of the young man but the killing of Elizabeth Jillian Adler, daughter of local developer James Adler. Miss Adler went missing a year ago in Aspen, Colorado, believed to be the victim of a skiing accident. However, with the murder of Mr. Patterson, evidence and a confession has come to light that shine a guilty verdict on Miss Markham. "State police of both Vermont and Colorado are carrying on the investigation," Sheriff Crew Turner said at yesterday's press conference. "With assistance from FBI and our own local forensics team."

The passing of Mr. Patterson couldn't have come on a worse night. Hailed as a fundraiser like no other and observed internationally by investors and fans of Reading alike, losing a son of the local powerhouse founding family during Mayor Olivia Walker's inaugural Valentine's Ball will have repercussions when it comes time to fill campaign promises. However, Mayor Walker insists this event will have no bearing on future developments. "Reading is a fantastic town, the best town in Vermont, the cutest town in America." At least, according to our enthusiastic mayor. "Funding partners are lining up to develop the area further and I have no doubt our progress will proceed on time and on budget."

It should be noted that esteemed businessman and noted developer, Emile Welter Ries of Luxembourg, while in attendance that night, has since pulled backing for further support of Reading's expansion in the tourism market according to a local source. With the loss of such a large funding partner, it's possible our mayor's dreams may be falling apart.

AND NOW FOR A peek at Book Three…

FAME AND FORTUNE AND MURDER

CHAPTER ONE

THERE WAS JUST SOMETHING spectacular about a hot latte and a deliciously sunny April morning that stirred my optimism. Not that I had anything to complain about, really, but the beaming sunshine and perfectly roasted and sugared aroma of fresh coffee mixed with the smiling relief of small town residents recently released from the depressing gray of winter put an extra bounce in my step.

Not just mine, either. As I passed through the glass doors of the most yummy smelling place in all of Reading, Vermont—who didn't adore the scent of well-brewed Colombian?—and into the warm and welcoming arms of Spring, I nodded with excellent humor to everyone who returned the grin I shared like we had some secret we'd long been keeping to ourselves and were only now beginning to pass around.

Even the air smelled of new beginnings, that particularly heavenly mix of freshness and damp earth mingling with the scent of crushed pine needles washing down from the mountains seemed to melt away the misery of the last three weeks. Now, allow me to be clear. We hadn't just come through Armageddon or six snowstorms in a row or even a hurricane. Instead, the twenty-one days of pretty much incessant rainfall had turned our entire quaint town into a damp and mildewing mud ball. I'd given up on any chance of getting into the garden at Petunia's, my bed and breakfast, before summer at that rate, each and every morning dragging me deeper into the gloom of misty patheticness fed by temperatures far too mild to even make snow.

And thanks to the loss of cold weather, tourism dried up to the point I only had one set of guests in my normally packed house, a pair of patiently kind grandparents who'd come from Florida to enjoy spring in Vermont. At least now they'd be able to emerge from their hideout in the carriage house Blue

Suite and explore town instead of spending endless hours playing our worn down Monopoly that I was positive was missing Boardwalk.

Petunia grunted next to me as she trotted along, doing her best to keep up. I'd spent the winter trying to regulate her diet and get her off the treats and sugar my best friend, Daisy, and own traitor mother had been sneaking her. But it was apparent either the pug named after my inherited business was finding ways to steal extra food or the two older ladies who worked for me were ignoring my orders not to give the dog anything not on her approved list. The post-it note stuck to the big stainless steel fridge had gone missing lately, I noticed, so I had a feeling it was the latter rather than the former.

"Don't think that donut hole you just ate is going to be a regular occurrence," I said, unable to resist the offer when the perky young woman handed over the sugary confection. Petunia's pathetic expression and bulging eyes showing the whites tweaked my heart strings and, I guess, the lovely day made me generous.

Petunia didn't even look up at me, likely plotting her next opportunity to bully someone into giving her food that made her flatulent. It wasn't so much her round belly that concerned me as it was her unfortunate habit of farting on me in her sleep. My attempt to kick her off the bed had failed completely and she'd been curled up next to me every night since I gave in. But if she was going to keep expelling that level of gas it was quite possible I'd go to bed one night and just never wake up.

Toxic pug gas slayed.

I skipped around a small stack of pylons and a long, low barrier of white painted lumber while my deputy cousin unloaded more of the same from the back of the sheriff's pickup. I beamed at Robert Carlisle, not because I adored him. Quite the opposite. I couldn't stand the wretched little piece of loathing with his seventies-esque bush of a black mustache or his pompous superiority that he got to be a cop and I didn't or his growing beer belly and hideous leer he liked to aim at any woman under the age of fifty. And the feeling was mutual, though none of the previous applied. I was sure Robert had his own list of things about me he despised, but I was positive his number one reason for hating my guts was the fact I was the daughter of former sheriff John Fleming and he would never, ever be.

No, I grinned and waved out of sheer delight at his less than enthusiastic expression as he grunted his way through hefting a rather heavy looking barricade onto the sidewalk.

"Exercise is good for you," I said as I kept going without offering to help.

"Your ass could use some lately, Fanny," he shot after me.

He did *not* just call me fat and Fanny in the same sentence. I spun back, good mood turned to snarling anger, and found Deputy Jillian Wagner smiling at me, shaking her head. Once I discovered Jill couldn't stand Robert either, I'd invited her over for coffee and her best advice hit me with that smile.

Do not engage the troll.

Instead, I paused next to her and completely ignored my cousin who glared at us. Jill took a break, her blonde ponytail tucked into the collar of her khaki uniform button up, white t-shirt showing at her collarbone. Nice to know another woman about my height, especially in Reading where everyone seemed to lean toward the petite side. While 5'7" wasn't gigantic, I sometimes felt like I towered over other women, including my elderly employees, Mary and Betty Jones. Made me feel a bit awkward.

"You staying around for the parade?" Jill's voice always surprised me, sweet and light, and from what I heard she was a hell of a soprano.

Oh, crap, right. I'd forgotten the parade. On purpose. "Ah," I said, looking down at my latte.

She laughed. "Gotcha. Gardening?" She sounded wistful.

I beamed a smile. "Can't wait to get into the beds now that the ground is drying out some. I might transfer some of the bushes but for now I'm going to clean up and prep for planting." If any of my old friends from my five years living in New York City could have heard me they'd have fallen off their designer platforms and spilled their own expensive and impossible to order coffees. A lot had changed since my Grandmother Iris died and left me Petunia's. Including two murders and a secret trail of clues that led me to a broken music box I was in the process of having restored.

"I'll pop over when I get the chance if that's okay?" Jill lifted a pile of orange cones from the back of the truck. "I'd love to get slips of the two bushes near the front steps if that's still all right?"

I grinned, nodded. "I'll be home all weekend," I said. "Avoiding the fanfare."

She wrinkled her nose, freckles coming together under her blue-gray eyes. Not many people I knew looked that good without makeup, her naturally dark lashes so thick I felt envy every time I looked at her. "Wish I could join that club," Jill said. "But it's all hands on deck this weekend."

I wasn't surprised. "Has Olivia been driving Crew nuts?" Ever since the weather turned and our tourist numbers with it our dear Mayor Walker had been slowly losing her mind. Her push to attract visitors had, so far, created a wave of new business for Reading and I was frankly impressed by her determination. While the whole grow or die mentality gave me the creeps, I couldn't complain about the benefits to my bank account.

But, as I looked around the busy main street of the place she'd coined as the "cutest town in America," I wondered if these past few weeks of quiet weren't a good thing. It had been nice to relax a little, put my feet up, get to some projects requiring my attention without feeling like I had to hurry or scurry or fudge the edges because I just didn't have time.

There was something to be said for a break in the crazy, especially with summer coming. And this weekend's activities were bound to stir things up again.

"Have Willow and Skip arrived yet?" The focal points of today's parade, Reading's most famous citizens, lived in Hollywood full time. But that didn't stop Olivia from shamelessly badgering the A-list star and her football hero husband to promote our town. Which, I thought, they'd done so far with grace and thoughtfulness, part of the reason Olivia's campaign to increase tourism had worked out so well. But this weekend's commercial filming following the pomp of a parade for the happy couple was just a bit much for my stomach.

Thus hiding in the garden in the sunshine and letting the rest of Reading deal.

"I think so," Jill said. "The sheriff and the mayor were driving to the airport to meet them at 9AM, so I assume they're back by now." Likely staying at the White Valley Ski Lodge in the penthouse suite. I personally preferred to avoid the place since almost dying on Valentine's Day and helping solve two murders. But it was a beautiful spot and the perfect refuge for the famous pair.

"Have fun," I said, waving to Jill and tossing my long, auburn hair at Robert who snarled back.

Petunia grumbled about walking as she always did, pausing now and then the two and a half blocks to the B&B just to see if I'd stop and pick her up. Which I refused to do.

"Maybe we both need more exercise," I said. Refused, of course, to believe Robert's cruel comment was anything but crap while a tiny part of me whispered I had been enjoying Betty's cooking a lot lately, not to mention my mother's amazing fare and hadn't I spent the winter working but not working out…? "That's it. We both need to shift our habits. What do you say?" Whether true or not— suck it, Robert—I missed my daily runs in the city. Time to take that up again.

Petunia didn't seem all that enthusiastic. I should have adopted a Labrador.

I looked up as I rounded the corner of Booker Street, heart stuttering while my smile faded and my lovely day of nothing but puttering in the garden took a massive turn for the oh crap now what. My normally quiet street, the odd car lining the sidewalks even when we were fully booked, now looked like a war zone. By the time I forced my sneakered feet past the stretch limo and the giant white van with the camera equipment, cables and lights and other things

I couldn't comprehend snaking and looming their intrusion on my life and the three hulking men in dark suits and earbuds with plastic wires running into their collars, I had a horrible, horrible feeling I wasn't in Kansas anymore.

Nope, I was in Reading, Vermont. Cutest town in America.

My desperate need to explain this mess away disappeared with the sudden appearance of Olivia bustling from my front door, hurrying down the steps and to my side where she stopped with a deep scowl and a determined look on her face. One hand lifted to grasp my elbow as she leaned in and hissed the following.

"The Lodge has a gas leak and you're all I have. So live with it." She beamed then, leaning away, voice rising to politician volume while I gaped at her. "Petunia's is the perfect place to house our special guests and staging ground for our parade. Historic and distinctly Reading, it's been a landmark in our sweet little town for decades. I just know our visitors will love it here." She tucked one arm around my shoulders, her dark red suit making me think of blood while I tried desperately to come up with something to say to stop this train wreck from happening. "Thank you so much to Fiona Fleming for being our most gracious host."

Wait, that sounded like a speech, didn't it? I looked away from her to find she'd been speaking to a camera. Of course she had and I stood there and stared at it like an idiot struck by lightning.

I knew then, like it or not, I was now a part of whatever Olivia had planned.

AUTHOR NOTES

I'm enamored with murder. But not the gory kind that makes you go "Ew" and scrunch your nose and feel sick. No, I'm totally and utterly wrapped up in the kind of slaying that gives me a detective curiosity thrill I'm only now uncovering after all this time.

Who knew I'd fall in love with killing people?

Writers are odd folk.

I honestly had no idea what to expect from writing cozy mysteries, but the more I explore the genre, the more at home I feel. In fact, I was meant to write book two of another series after finishing Chocolate Hearts and Murder and, instead, when I penned chapter one of Fame and Fortune and Murder and realized just how tied to Fiona I'd become, I begged for you, the reader, to be patient and let me stay in Reading for just one more book.

I'll get back to Ethie and Syd and Miriam and the Hayle Coven Universe in short order. In about a week, actually. But it's been such a delight to spend time in the cutest town in America I just can't bring myself to leave yet.

That being said, while originally I thought there were twelve (and then thirteen) books in the Fiona

Fleming Cozy Mystery series, I'm realizing just how much more she has to say. So, we'll see. For now, I'm going to hang out at Petunia's, put up with pug farts and help Fee figure out, yet again, whodunit.

All my best in murder and mayhem,

Patti

ABOUT THE AUTHOR

EVERYTHING YOU NEED TO know about me is in this one statement: I've wanted to be a writer since I was a little girl, and now I'm doing it. How cool is that, being able to follow your dream and make it reality? I've tried everything from university to college, graduating the second with a journalism diploma (I sucked at telling real stories), was in an all-girl improv troupe for five glorious years (if you've never tried it, I highly recommend making things up as you go along as often as possible). I've even been in a Celtic girl band (some of our stuff is on YouTube!) and was an independent film maker. My life has been one creative thing after another—all leading me here, to writing books for a living.

Now with multiple series in happy publication, I live on beautiful and magical Prince Edward Island (I know you've heard of Anne of Green Gables) with my very patient husband and six massive cats.

I love-love-love hearing from you! You can reach me (and I promise I'll message back) at patti@pattilarsen.com. And if you're eager for your next dose of Patti Larsen books (usually about one release a month) come join my mailing list! All the best up and coming, giveaways, contests and, of course, my observations on the world (aren't you just dying to know what I think about everything?) all in one place: http://smarturl.it/PattiLarsenEmail.

Last—but not least!—I hope you enjoyed what you read! Your happiness is my happiness. And I'd love to hear just what you thought. **A review** where you found this book would mean the world to me—**reviews feed writers** more than you will ever know. So, loved it (or not so much), **your honest review** would make my day. **Thank you!**

88363633R00187

Made in the USA
Lexington, KY
10 May 2018